The Welsh Ma

Also by Dave Lewis:

Layer Cake © 2009
Urban Birdsong © 2010
Sawing Fallen Logs For Ladybird Houses © 2011
Welsh Poetry Competition Anthology © 2011
Ctrl-Alt-Delete © 2011
Haiku © 2012
Raising Skinny Elephants © 2013
Roadkill © 2013
Photography Composition © 2014
iCommand © 2015
Land's End to John o' Groats © 2015
Reclaiming the Beat © 2016
Wales Trails © 2016
Welsh Poetry Competition Anthology II © 2016
Happy © 2017
Basic Photoshop © 2017
Going Off Grid © 2018
Never Seventeen © 2018
Hadrian's Cycleway & C2C © 2019
Scratching The Surface © 2019

Websites:

www.david-lewis.co.uk
www.poetrybookawards.co.uk
www.welshpoetry.co.uk
www.publishandprint.co.uk
www.wales-trails.co.uk
www.welshwriters.co.uk

The Welsh Man

Dave Lewis

Publish & Print
www.publishandprint.co.uk

Special thanks to Catrin Collier and Sue Gurman for their helpful comments, suggestions, edits and continued support

Front cover image: Artem Saranin
Back cover image & design: Dave Lewis
Back cover author photograph: Dave Jones

"It seems to me most strange that men should fear;
Seeing that death, a necessary end,
Will come when it will come."

- Shakespeare

To the good guys

One

Autumn 2004

The sun was blood red in a vast blue sky. The sea was flat with the occasional sparkle of white. The light spun slowly, kaleidoscoping through coral pink and orange peel before finally settling into a sickly Indian burgundy. It wasn't the worst day to die.

As I ambled back from the beach, hands in pockets, head down, the last rays of September filtered through the gaps in the shabby, dirty buildings reminding me how a toothy grin might occasionally shine on an alcoholic's leathered face. For once I actually felt pretty good.

Soon the darkness would spread its cloak over the remains of the day though. In a few minutes I wouldn't know anything else at all, ever. If I was being honest with myself I'd been lucky to have lasted this long. But I suppose the timing could have been better.

Yeh, that was it. I just wanted a few more days. Time enough to settle all the things a condemned man felt needed to be sorted. Another year would have been good. I began to chuckle to myself at the thought as I crossed the deserted car park behind the faded splendour of the Pier Hotel.

The light was dying faster now. The heavens slowly blackened. Soon it would be totally black. Blacker than it had ever been before. Ah fuck it, what the hell. I stared impassively at the long barrel protruding out of the dark. I grimaced as a small, solitary black cloud rose behind the hooded figure that stepped silently out of the shadows.

The silhouette stopped ten feet away from me. Not close enough for me to reach him in time, not far enough away for him to miss. I recognised his professionalism. That's where I would have stood.

'Go on then, get it over with,' I said.

Two

I was originally from the valleys; that fabled area of south Wales that fanned out north from the coastal cities of Cardiff and Newport. A place of tight-knit, working-class communities that inhabited the rows of picture-postcard, multi-coloured terraced houses fastened to the sides of scarred and coal-blackened mountains.

I lived on an estate, affectionately known as "top site", which was plonked on top of a hill that used to be on an ancient pilgrim's trail back around Jesus' time.

Mam rented a small three-bedroomed house from the council. It was built in the sixties and already past its prime. Painted a sickly off-cream colour, the paint cracked and waning. We only had a small front garden but a large back one. Overgrown with three-foot weeds, brambles and an old fridge no-one ventured out there much. Certainly not my old man, who was far too busy on the fiddle or drinking in the innumerable local pubs to worry about a spot of landscape gardening.

*

I guess I was about fifteen or sixteen when my dad had raised his hands to the old girl one too many times. It coincided with me realising how hard I could hit. Not that I wanted to take any chances though, 'cos he was a solid bastard too. I took a frying pan to his face and smashed his nose in.

He stuck around for a few days afterwards but then he moved out for good.

A few mornings after the attack I remember he crept silently towards my bedroom, although he didn't dare walk in. He just stood there, framed in the doorway, like a rat tasting the air.

Cars were bleating their horns outside and seeing my eyes were open he raised his hands in mock surrender and spoke to me for the last time.

'I'm off son.'

'Okay.'

'I just wanted to say… goodbye,' he stuttered.

'Aye.' I replied.

He fidgeted a bit but wasn't that sure of himself. He saw the breadknife I had within arms reach, sticking out from under the mattress, and I think he knew I'd use it.

'Look, I'm sorry you had to see me slapping mam about…' he paused to look at me. 'It's just that…'

'Yeh?' I demanded.

His voice softened.

'One day you'll understand.'

He continued to confess his sins to me for a few minutes. He said he'd had a lot to put up with, that I had no idea how infuriating she was and hoped that one day we'd be cool about it all. Said he didn't expect me to forgive him but hoped that quite soon I'd do the same thing as he was doing and I'd leave the festering valleys for good.

'Get away up to London son or pop across the bridge to Bristol eh. Somewhere away from all this bloody decay,' he advised.

Staring at him, I was unsure what he wanted me to say or do.

'Alright, I'm off then, ta ra,' he said, like he was just popping down the Spar for a six-pack of tinnies. I sensed he was afraid of the silence and it was then I noticed a dreadful look of longing on his ugly, bruised face.

Of course, back then I had no idea what he was talking about so I just nodded and gave him a half-smile. He wasn't such a bad bloke I guess and mam couldn't half scream abuse at him when she was tanked up on cheap cider.

Extending my hand I shot him with my fingers, then instantly regretted it. I only meant it as a joke and that I'd see him around. Shit. Did he think I was going to get him? I hoped not, family is family after all. You had to stick by your family, even if you hated them sometimes. And mam and dad was all I had in those days.

Sat up in bed, I pulled my blanket over my shoulders as my breath came out in little clusters of white smoke.

'Bye dad,' I just about managed to shout as his shadow melted from the doorway.

Pulling the curtains open I watched his shape get smaller and smaller until he disappeared over the brow of the hill. I willed him to stop, turn around and wave. He never did. A woman yelled at a dog that had found something interesting to sniff. She tugged hard on the lead but the huge, scabby pit bull wasn't having none of it.

The dog seemed happy enough. I heard my dad ended up in Newcastle or somewhere near there.

As far back as I could remember I was always known as a bit of a tough guy. After leaving school I'd played rugby for one of the hardest clubs in the district and nobody messed with me on or off the pitch. Not unless they wanted their face kicked in anyway. Even my older, more experienced teammates quickly learnt to give me a wide berth. And in the local nightclubs, late on a Saturday evening, it was worse.

Soon I had a reputation not just in our valley but also the next two. Violence had always been there. Simmering under the surface, ready to erupt for no apparent purpose. Although if you'd asked me back then I would have told you there was always a very reasonable excuse for my ferocious outbursts.

"Get your punishment in first" I remember my old man telling me. About the only bit of useful advice I could ever remember getting from him.

Sure, I lived life on the edge but there was always a sort of code amongst the boys. There had to be a line you wouldn't cross. A point where you said no, that's enough. A place you wouldn't go or you just ended up being as bad as them. With me it was drug dealers. I hated them. That world had always seemed a sinister place to me, one that was best avoided.

My standards weren't high by any means but they were what they were. And it certainly paid dividends to find that out if you ever intended to walk down the same street as me without getting a pasting. Like many of my contemporaries I'd learnt the hard way and my, albeit questionable ethics were ingrained in me like the dirt in the creases of my fingerprints.

So the bottom line was no pushers could ever expect leniency. They choose their bed and I'd make them lie in it. Although crawl face down, or perhaps drown in their own blood, might have been more apt.

I always used to say to people, don't accept all that crap about there being no other way. That they grew up in a shithole council flat and had to watch their old dear injecting, getting off their face on vodka or whatever. So it was inevitable they'd end up a junkie - yeh right! Same old, same old. The stuck record, the pathetic bullshit about there being no decent jobs around and the government was to blame.

That just because they were six years old when they had to steady the dull bitch's hand, hold the needle still, find a willing vein and guide her to bed afterwards it wasn't their fault. Nah, I didn't buy it at all and always used to believe you weren't forced to put that poison into you, not if you didn't want to anyway. You just needed a bit of self-respect. You always had a choice I reckoned.

Well, that's how I used to think. Before I met her.

Three

There was a fog of tobacco smoke hovering above the bar. The old television set, high above the door in the corner, had Maggie's smug face on it, telling us we'd never had it so good or some other bullshit. Nobody noticed until an old retired miner sprang off his stool, swore at the screen and switched channels.

The lights from the pumps shone through the gloom and lit up Jamie John, small-time hoodlum in the making and local pretty boy. He was holding court at the back of the dirty, dilapidated pub, a small entourage of low life hanging on his monosyllabic, X-rated grunts. My pissed up mother was bending over the pool table. I watched out of the corner of my eye as he started to rub his filthy hands up and down my mam's arse – one too many times for my liking.

The jukebox was playing an old Tom Jones track and a gang of middle-aged women who'd clearly overdone the war paint were howling along in the seats opposite the bar. I rose from my seat at the end of the counter and moved in without thinking.

He saw me coming alright, I was hard to miss, but he just grinned like a fuckin' retard and carried on caressing mam's ripped Levis. His out-and-out arrogance wound me up even more.

Jamie John was habitually coked up and full of the usual bravado that went with it. He didn't think I'd mix it up with him, not now it was common knowledge he was

16

hooked up with the heroin pushers involved in the growing and extremely profitable drug trade down in Swansea. He thought he was a gangster. Untouchable. What a dickhead.

Mam turned around, blocking my way and gave me a fake smile. 'No babe, don't bother, it's alright. He was just joking mun. Leave him alone.'

I didn't reply but just looked through her.

'Calm down love, he was only playing mun. You know what he's like.'

A mother knew her own son. And she was looking at red mist. She'd first seen it when I'd flattened the old man, a few years earlier. She knew what was brewing beneath my calm exterior and I think it scared her a little.

The cocky twat was still smirking as I slowly walked towards him, my head and shoulders sagging like I wasn't really aware of him. I put a protective arm around my mam and slowly turned her away, smiling to her gently but secretly seething inside.

'Yeh, no worries mam,' I bent down to whisper reassuringly in her ear. Then I let my arm casually drop from her back and turned to face him. The edges of my being were starting to fray.

Up until then he'd watched my approach in silence. Then he opened his mouth to speak, to say something derisive or maybe even threaten me. He had a small audience around the pool table now. People that would later be witnesses at my trial.

Without saying a word I punched straight and fast. Seventeen stone of muscle behind that first blow caused his left eye to immediately swell up and close. He rocked on his feet for a split-second, then staggered back two paces with the impact of the first strike as the second hit him on his chin. A glancing left hook as he was already on his way to the floor. I quickly followed up by kicking him between the legs. He half-heartedly clutched at his testicles through his tight, skinny jeans but he was already barely conscious. I should have walked away. If I had that would possibly have been the end of it but I saw the cue ball within easy reach and instinctively picked it up, calmly knelt down to his level and slowly and methodically proceeded to knock his front teeth out with it.

Looking back on those early, wild days, I guess it was just a matter of time before I took a short vacation at her majesty's pleasure. I was convicted of GBH, which I later learned is a criminal offence under Sections 18 and 20 of the Offences Against the Person Act. I got three years even though it was a first offence. Apparently, I "might have gone a bit over the top" if I was to quote my defence solicitor. The snooty beak, who didn't even know me, branded me a "nasty piece of work". I guess she must have been a good judge of character after all.

*

This was about twenty odd years back, half my life ago. By the time I got out of prison I had learnt a few more tricks and was more than ready to leave south Wales.

I'd met guys inside from all over the south west, a couple of them had mentioned the big cities, said it was better than the backward villages most of us came from. They said there was real money to be made, especially if you weren't afraid to get your hands dirty. I certainly wasn't afraid of that. So I guess it was inevitable that I just drifted into it.

When they let me out of prison I considered hopping straight on the InterCity 125 to London there and then but some invisible phantom dragged me back to the valleys. Like everyone I got sucked back in.

I reasoned with myself – figuring I should check on mam first. I also realised that to get properly back on my feet I would have to get some cash behind me before I split. I couldn't live on fresh air could I?

Leaping off the red and white bus I decided to take a stroll along the riverbank. I noticed the usual sooty-dark waters were much clearer than when I'd been growing up and everyone had jobs.

Stopping briefly to listen to a blackbird sing its beautiful song seemed incongruous as I negotiated the drab, post-industrial wasteland all around me. I kicked a polystyrene chip carton into the filthy gutter and then saw an old woman throw a bowl of soapy-grey dishwater onto the pavement, narrowly missing the local vicar as he hopped, skipped and jumped past her door. I turned uphill towards the estate with a smile on my face.

I observed a fat, teenage mother with a baby clamped to her hip swigging from a can of Special Brew. It was about ten o'clock in the morning. When I reached the ramshackle house I went in through the unlocked back door.

'Shwmae mam,' echoed through the empty kitchen.

I noticed the sink full of piled up tea mugs and

food-stained plates. It smelt like a family of mice had taken up residence in there. I continued into the hallway. The telly was on loud in the front room. A ragged collection of cloth animals were singing a song about a cat. The curtains were drawn even though it was light outside and a single photograph of mam and dad stared back at me from the mantelpiece above the gas fire. The glass in the frame was cracked like a spider's web. On the floor next to the record player were a pile of vinyl LPs. Heaped haphazardly the album sleeves had brown ring stains from beer cans all over them. The album *A Night At The Opera* by Queen stared back at me.

It was then I heard a low moaning coming from upstairs and the ceiling above me seemed to be moving. I knew dad wouldn't have come back so reasoned she had someone new to buy her drink these days. After throwing a few things in a bag I left the same way I'd come in and never saw my mam again.

I heard years later that she'd been killed in a hit and run on the site. Boy racers doing drag races up and down the road. She'd stepped off the pavement, lashed up of course, at the wrong time. Died instantly apparently.

Retracing my steps, back downhill to the village I noticed the thick grime on the windows, the boarded up shops and the plum-coloured noses of old men that I pass. People had a ghost-like appearance, pale as the rain.

In prison everyone had been fed three times a day and we even had a decent sized gym. The place might have been awash with drugs but there was no alcohol. I got fitter and stronger. It was like a deluxe health club compared to living in this dead place and only then did I realise it.

Although I was never good at much in school I did like reading. Inside I took the habit back up again. I loved travel books and biographies. A bit of history too. I'd never been anywhere but always wanted to. I had a passport but wasn't sure if it was out of date.

I spent the rest of the day in the pub. I bumped into an old friend, Mike, in the De Winton, who'd just come over from the other valley for a pint.

'How many people have I told what it's like here?' I asked.

'Yeh butt, you do go on a bit. There are the locals of course - the ones who'll listen anyway. But then I guess they already know the score,' said Mike.

'There was that voluptuous, blonde exchange student from Italy. I took her around the back of the grandstand, up the rugby ground, but instead of sweet nothings I ended up preaching politics at her.'

'Heh, what are you like?'

'And last year, down the international. There was those Aussie backpackers we got chatting to, remember?'

'They never listened though. Always thought they had a better story and they made sure they told us so!'

'Yeh, wankers,' I laughed.

'And all those English rugby teams, in the clubhouse after a game...'

'Ah shit yeh, I do don't I?'

'Aye well, this was once the heart of industrial Wales,' Mike impersonated me.

'Fuck off.'

And continuing the lecture…

'This region has played such a massive part in world history see. The coal, iron and steel that was mined and produced here fuelled an empire that helped Great Britain win two world wars.'

'Okay, I get it, shut up before I slap you.'

'You and who's army?'

'Cheers mate.' I clinked Mike's glass with mine.

It was true though. The agreeing nods only lasted so long. It was my malediction. The more I ranted and raved, the quicker people left me. Usually alone at a bar, nursing a pint of flat pale ale.

It was certainly true that since the relative prosperity of the sixties and seventies had evaporated, and the spectre of Thatcherism reared its ugly head through the eighties, there were only two courses of action open to youngsters who were born in the valleys. Depending on your viewpoint, you could either live and die there in relative misery and obscurity or grow some balls and get out.

Opinions change with experience though. Most people who reminisce do so optimistically – they tend to leave out the bad bits.

If you spoke to me now I'd tell you it wasn't such a bad place to be brought up. Most people were friendly and there was a certain resilience. The valleys left a mark on you for sure and I've certainly inherited the sick sense of humour and extraordinary spirit about the place. Deprivation and hardship became a badge of belonging. You know what I mean? Everyone's had to suffer something; otherwise you wouldn't fit in.

After stop tap I grabbed a bag of chips then crashed at my mate Dai's flat.

'I tell you, it's crazy the way people behave.'

'Ow da ya mean?' answered Dai.

'Well think about it. Generations of folk have left here before right?'

'Aye butt.'

'So why the fuck do they come back? I mean, some of them literally can't wait like!'

'You can take the boy out of the valley but you can't take the valley out of the boy.'

'Aye, true. Very eloquent Dai.'

'I get what you mean though. Fair enough if you go up to London and make your fortune. Come back here and you're a millionaire like.'

'Yeh, but if all you know is getting burgled. You know – if you live up top site. House broken into a dozen times. Why would you still reckon you love it here?'

'S'right. A mate of mine used to live there. He got his car pinched. Scumbags smashed it up, then set fire to it. He was always getting terrorised by the addicts and hooligans...'

'I fuckin' hate the druggies butt.'

I touched Dai's tin and he smirked.

'Cheers.'

*

Looking back I guess we all had the same love-hate relationship with the place. Eventually though the poverty, drugs, low-waged jobs and political stagnation took their toll on most of the towns and villages I knew. It was sad but inevitable.

I suppose I always knew I'd leave. It was just a matter of when. I was looking for a different version of myself. A better one anyway. Typically for me, like so many others before me, it was when all hope had checked out.

By seven the next morning I was up and showered and heading for the bus stop. I chased away a young lad that was urinating in the shelter and noticed a used needle on the pavement.

To find a decent job I would have to head to the city. I figured the valleys were out unless I fancied freezing my nuts off doing scaffolding or roofing over Christmas.

As the bus approached I gazed back up at the estate. Ghostly wisps of grey cloud circled around the mountain obscuring the blocks of flats from view. Without warning the air felt different. The heavens snapped and crackled and blue light lit up a lilac sky. I jumped on the bus and never looked back.

*

Heading to Cardiff, the capital city of Wales, I got a job the first day. I walked around all the construction sites and asked for work. It was easy. No paperwork to fill in, no certificates or checks, all the foreman cared about was how hard you worked. All cash in hand too. I stayed on a friend's settee in Riverside until I saved enough for a bond on a rental.

The Welsh capital in the mid-eighties was an

interesting place to be with lots of swanky new developments shooting up everywhere. The old replaced by the new, with various gangsters and crooked businessmen vying for position doing dodgy property deals, especially down the old docks.

In contrast to the valley towns there was always plenty of labour too. I began my time doing a few stints on the buildings. I was a hod carrier on the original Holiday Inn site. At first we got paid by the brick. The more you could hump to the brickies at the top of the ever-growing skyscraper the more you got paid – a health and safety devoid area that was a recipe for disaster of course.

We all used to stack way too many bricks on and inevitably a few would slip out from under the protective mesh and fall off as you climbed the high ladders. One guy even got killed when a small red house brick fell thirteen floors, smashed his skull in and made pizza out of his brain.

We got the day off when that happened.

'That'll teach him not to wear his hard hat,' joked Lawrence, my workmate at the time.

'Yeh, shame eh. It'll be a big insurance pay out, the foreman said.'

'Whose round is it?'

'I'll get them mate.'

'Think they're covered for a million quid, which works out at about one death per year...'

'Stella aye?'

Following that accident they tightened up a bit on us labourers so we decided to swap weight for speed. We used to see how fast we could get to the top of the site instead. It was about this time that I discovered some blokes would bet on anything. Two flies walking down a pane of glass or two stupid valley boys sprinting up a ladder with sixty plus pounds of house bricks on their shoulders. I can't say I was a fan of heights but they didn't scare me too much either. Especially as my morning coffee was usually laced with a fair few shots of whisky to take the edge off and give me a bit of Dutch courage for the day ahead.

One positive side effect of that kind of graft was that my arms, shoulders and leg muscles became absolutely huge after working there for six months, hunched against the strong wind as you climbed up and down.

After witnessing a few more nasty accidents though I soon realised a building site was a dangerous place to work full-time. When I got more regular work I gave it up.

I ended up spending a couple of years in the fast-changing city. I mainly did door work on the club circuit. It wasn't bad work, especially after I learnt you could get much further being nice to people than bashing them.

'Empathy, that's what it's all about mate,' said Nick, an uncompromising doorman from Newport who was also a fifth Dan at karate and my mentor in those early days.

Cardiff in the eighties was good fun too. There was a great mix of places to hang out. Snazzy new clubs and bars were springing up all over the metropolis. You also had all the old Brains pubs, with the city's illustrious and often roguish history still well and truly alive inside them.

I soon learned the best places to meet folks, where to pick up a few quid's worth of counterfeit notes and where to get a slightly warm Fred Perry polo shirt. I also discovered where the local Cardiff crews hung out and perhaps more importantly which waterholes to avoid, unless you fancied a wee scrap. It was a good time to be in the city.

I even met a girl. A girl that would change my life – for better and for worse, as the saying goes.

Four

Charley was a beautiful blonde. Long wavy hair tumbled down over her shoulders. Deep brown eyes with a hint of self-preservation if you looked hard enough and a small, elfin body with understated curves in all the right places.

It was about ten o'clock on a Friday night. The club was quiet by normal weekend standards. It was one of the weeks in between Six Nations internationals so the townies were out en masse as opposed to the die-hard sports fans and the valley women making the year's great expedition, via a thirty or forty-minute train ride, into the hedonistic, yet still incredibly alien, city centre.

'Not tonight mate, we're full.'

'Ah, I think my friend is in there butt,' mumbles this drunk homeless guy.

I'm stood on the door as he tries to push past me but I stop him with one arm.

'Slow down buttie bach, you're not coming in tonight. Anyway, I think I saw your mate turn down Park Place so you'd best try there or maybe Queen Street.'

He stops and stares at me for a few brief seconds. He has no concept of the fact that I've offered him two completely opposite directions to go in. It's then I notice his eyes and realise he's not sloshed but off his face on some shit. He might be plastered as well though for all I know or care. Fuckin' druggies everywhere in those days.

He sizes me up for a short while then grins, attempts to shake my hand and wanders off. Pausing at the wrought-iron gates at the boundary of the club he starts fumbling in his pockets for a cigarette and I can see the large, red neon club sign reflecting off his grey, sunken face.

'Have a good night sir,' my sarcasm fluent at this time of night.

It was then I spotted her. She stood out a mile because she had a long, faux-fur coat on while her three friends were all half naked in miniskirts and flimsy tops. A covering of goose pimples due to the cold, impractical high heels and hunched shoulders completed the look as they shivered away, desperate to get in somewhere before the big queues started. Charley approached me first.

'Alright handsome, what's it like inside then?'

'Warmer,' I reply with a smile, indicating her friends. 'Come on in then.'

She reflects a smile far too quickly and I'm immediately thinking about what's under the coat. AK47 or just a Dooney & Bourke full of pills.

'Can I check your bags girls?' I ask.

The pause is too long by a fraction of a second and so I know she's got something on her she shouldn't.

The others quickly barge in front and rush to show me their open purses like they do this every time they go in anywhere.

Letting them in first, I then stop Charley.

'I have to ask love, sorry.'

She throws a selfie-like pose at me as her coat becomes a bat cape in the chilly night air and I immediately zoom in to her hard nipples poking through a thin top. Slowly but deliberately she starts to show me her large handbag like you would at airport customs.

I don't bother looking, it's probably just speed or downer disco-biscuits.

'You planning on staying all night?' I ask with a wink. The perks of doing the door.

She drops her guard, undresses me with her eyes in two-seconds flat and then makes up her mind just as fast.

'Yeh, I'll wait for you big boy.'

*

The night dragged on slowly. I helped a few drunk lads off the dance floor, checked the gents a few times, noticed the tell-tale white lines etched into the top of the toilet seats. Adjusted my strap-on dicky bow in the mirror one too many times, smoothed down what was left of my close-cropped, number two hairstyle then went to the kitchen for a sandwich and a glass of Pepsi.

Virtually all pubs and nightclubs now have a big visible sign that nobody reads and certainly nobody bothers to adhere to. It says: "Anyone found with illegal drugs will be immediately removed from the premises and the police informed".

The bouncers know the clubs are swimming with drugs, the punters know, the dealers know, the manager knows and of course the cops know. Nobody does anything though. There is just too much money to be made and it's too much hassle to try to stop it. Everyone knows this except the poor, law-abiding parents of the unfortunate sods that get poisoned every weekend. The mothers and fathers you see on the telly, crying their eyes out on a floral settee after their ill-fated kids have overdosed and died in a pool of vomit in the back of a taxi or alone in an alleyway in a cold, wet, uncaring city. That's progress I suppose.

*

There's over two hundred people in the nightclub now, most of them swaying about, almost in time, to the state-of-the-art stereo system, many high as kites on class A and B. Thousands of pounds worth of sedatives, poppers and powder washing around.

Normally I'm on the lookout for the cocky bastards who think they can openly deal or use in plain view. I don't mind those nipping off to the bogs for a quick pill or a snort, the ones who show you a bit of respect by trying to hide the fact but the blatant twats need showing who's boss once in a while.

Seeing them use on the dance floor really annoys me so I'll grab them, throw them out and confiscate their stash. Most people take stuff before they come in anyway, it's just a matter of timing it well.

Then I spot her. She's on the dance floor with the one friend who's left without a stalker. The pulsating green and blue lights of the club are illuminating her golden hair and I stare mesmerised as she appears to turn jade then black and back again. Her flawless skin is flushed now from the exertion of dancing and she has a warm glow all around her.

Her other two companions are still in the club, a few feet away playing tonsil tennis with two sinewy wide boys. Matching chinos, Miami Vice t-shirts and jackets with wallets sticking out the arse pocket just begging to be lifted. Cloned knobheads skating over the sprung floor in shitty loafers. For a minute I'm almost jealous.

Charley catches me looking at her for far too long, which makes me think she's not had too much to drink so far. I feel a little embarrassed, letching at her like that. I start my rounds, telling the good ladies of the disco that it's time to drink up and bugger off outside. Into the freezing night to dribble curry and chips down their best frocks, get knocked over or molested by a Somali taxi driver or perhaps attempt to coax an erection out of a pissed-up clubber from Llanrumney.

Hovering at her table I watch as she makes sure her girlfriends' are all sorted and then she turns towards me and smiles.

'You live far then handsome?'

'House in Grangetown, car in the multi-storey,' I reply and walk away, trying to play it cool but also aware that Nick will need some backup as we tease and cajole the dregs out the door.

It always pays to get the girls out first. That way there's no reason for the lads to want to hang around.

A black guy with an open-neck white shirt and gold medallion decides he doesn't want to leave. He makes a lunge at Nick. Extremely bad move. The head bouncer quickly dipped out of the way and grabs the bloke's arm, bending it swiftly behind his back. He marches the man out the door, accidentally digs him under the ribs and throws him into the street. Nick gives him a stare that would break rocks.

'That's assault you cunt. You're a racist twat, I'll have you arrested,' screams the guy who tries to do an impression of an angry Richard Roundtree from the film Shaft but instead ends up looking like Bob Marley after someone stole his weed.

'Fuck off you black bastard before I step outside,' replies Nick as I close up alongside him, then sniggering to myself as I realise that Nick is a half-caste himself!

That was the thing with Cardiff in those days. It was a true melting pot. There were people from all over the world – Yemini, Italians, Greeks, Jews and loads from the Caribbean of course. Everyone mixed in pretty much okay. Although having said that, you wouldn't want to have a knife fight with a Maltese.

Yes, there was the odd bit of bother but it was usually 'cos someone was a twat, not 'cos they had different colour skin to you or anything. No-one seemed to notice most of the time. It was a bit of an eye-opener for me, being from the predominately white monoculture of the valleys. At first I wasn't sure what to call people but after a while you just said the first thing that came into your head and if it was wrong or you upset someone they'd just tell you and you'd say sorry. No hassle.

'The ability to express anger is especially important if you're a doorman,' advised Nick.

'What if they don't back down though mate?'

'Well, you have to be prepared to go all the way if a showy scrote fancies his chances, or hers for that matter, but generally most people are fine.'

'So I guess it's a balancing act,' I replied.

'Aye buttie boy. And restraint of course, you need that in bucketsful.'

I learnt a lot from Nick, if only I'd known him growing up.

You also have to have a sense of humour and be willing to stop yourself filling in the well-oiled arsehole who's being totally unreasonable and really asking for it. After all, he'd probably apologise if you saw him again the next day, sober. "Drink in, sense out", as my dear old mother used to say.

*

When everyone, except Charley, is finally out, the staff all sit around the bar and have one on the house. A reward for getting through the shift in tact I presume. I knock my ever-ready brandy back in one go and feel the reassuring warming sensation in the back of my throat. I usually get the barmaids to stick a double at the back of the counter for me, in case I need a quick shot of Dutch courage for a big scrap. Charley sips a whisky and coke then eyes me up and down again. Just to double-check I assume.

She's about five or six years older than me and now I've got a better chance to study her up close I can see she is well and truly in her prime – she's mature, confident and incredibly sexy.

In all honesty I'm utterly mesmerised by her. I watch her trace a beer stain ring with a long fingernail. The way her hand moves across the table, the way she wets her lips, how she crosses and uncrosses her long legs… everything. Fuckin' everything she does turns me on wicked.

'My girlfriends told me to stay away from you,' she said. How many times had she rehearsed this one in her mind?

'But here you are,' I answered.

'They all reckon you look dangerous,' she continued.

'Nah, he's a pussycat lovely,' said Nick smirking.

'P'raps she's got a thing for Neanderthals,' says one of the barmaids.

Charley toyed with the ice in her drink, making a show of it.

'Leave it out, he's a regular cutie I reckon.'

'She's looking for an adventure I think,' chips in one of the other girls.

Charley isn't fazed one bit by the banter and as the rest of the crowd start chatting amongst themselves I notice she has uncrossed her legs to reveal the bright scarlet silk flag of her knickers.

I get caught staring again.

'Right, come on then Tarzan, show me your tree-house.' Everyone laughs and looks at me.

'Okay, okay, let's go.' I'm delighted to oblige and reach for my jacket on the back of my stool.

We say our goodbyes to the others, walk out the side entrance into the car park stairwell and are soon sat in my beat-up, six-year old Ford Escort. Charley leans across and kisses me on the cheek as I turn the heating dial towards red and fire the ignition.

'I don't even know your name handsome?' she

asks.

'Paul.'

Five

She moved in to my place a week later. We'd spend half the day in bed, we ate takeaways far too often and when I trained at the nearby sports centre I couldn't wait to finish my routine so I could go back home and drag her into the shower with me. I was in a constant, near-religious state of arousal. We were like two batteries, charging each other.

It wasn't a great area, the houses were nice enough but many of them had seen better days. Summer or winter there would be windows wide open in the street. Reggae music blared out most hours of the day and night while a sickly, sweet smell of marijuana filled the air. There was rubbish piled up in black plastic bags, half of them split-open by seagulls, the others ransacked by the odd lurcher or Staffie cross that happened to be passing.

I rarely took girls back to my place and found myself apologising to Charley for the state of the tribal neighbourhood.

'Don't fret lover boy, it's filthy people who create slums no-one else.'

'Aye you have a point I suppose.'

We went out nearly every night. Tried every pub from Adamsdown to Cathays, laughed at the students dressed in Oxfam clothes, made friends with the locals and were soon on first-name terms with the owners of all the Indian and Chinese restaurants in the city.

After my work on Friday and Saturday nights we'd sleep in late then go for walks around Roath Park Lake on a Sunday afternoon. I used to smile at Charley; cloth boots over faded jeans, woolly jumper and duffle coat, swinging a half-empty bag of stale bread by her side. Her cinnamon eyes peaking out from underneath a train driver's cap.

The sky filling her golden face we'd stroll through weeping willow tunnels, avoid the swans hissing their disapproval before grabbing an ice lolly from the ever-present truck.

'Makes a change?' I say.

'What?'

'Getting actual vanilla from a van.'

'You've lost me love?'

'Well, back up the valley you're more likely to get a bag of smarties, know what I mean? And boxes of fags from Calais or a crate of ale that got pinched from the bottlers.'

'Ah, I get you. Yes, well this is the nicer part of the city init. Just raspberry ripple here babe.'

It was like we were normal people. It was a wonderful time and about the only real period in my life that I remember being truly happy.

I'd never had a proper relationship with anyone before and I was floating around on cloud nine all day long.

I even started to get nervous at work. Not sloppy exactly but I just didn't want to be there, in harms way. All I wanted to do was curl up in bed and have her teach me stuff I'd only read about in dirty magazines on building sites up until then.

Maybe I was getting soft?

Charley wasted no time in turning my modest few rooms into an extremely homely dwelling. She picked up my clothes off the floor and put them in the wardrobe, she cooked us food I'd never heard of and even bought a few cushions and throws to brighten the living room up a bit.

I loved to listen to her stories about growing up in London, or the big smoke as she called it. She told me about seeing men fighting in the streets, of men being bundled into vans and no one ever seeing them again. It all seemed especially thrilling to me, although I should really have been scared.

'One night daddy didn't come home. Mum cried all night, it was awful.'

'What happened?' I asked, hanging on her every word as always.

'I dunno.'

'You must do? You can tell me love.'

'Look, all I know is that it had something to do with an argument with a local Irish gang!'

She went on even though I could tell she was filling up with tears.

'Sorry, I didn't mean to…'

'Mum didn't want to talk about it. The next morning I was sent off to school as normal but when I got home the house had been cleared and my mum had two suitcases packed.'

'Where did you go?'

'By 'ere mun.' She was teasing me about my accent.

Charley continued, 'I was only allowed to choose one toy to bring with me before we rushed to the train station and came to Wales.'

'What toy did you bring?' I tried unsuccessfully to

lighten the mood.

'A cuddly rabbit named Eric, you dick.'

'Sorry.'

'We had tickets to Newport but mum kept us on until Cardiff. She had to plead with the guard to let us through the gate at Central station, saying we'd fallen asleep, didn't have any money, were running away from a violent past and that we were homeless. She was a good liar, mum. Unfortunately, it was all true.'

I put my muscular arm around Charley and squeezed her close to me while she continued to blurt out her harrowing and tragic life story.

'My mum was extremely resourceful though and soon got us a council flat, then she started a cleaning job, cash in hand of course, to top up our meagre benefits.'

'How old were you when this was all going on?' I asked.

'I think I was about fourteen then and it was 1971. I was brought up in Islington before the mad dash down 'ere. When we got here we settled in Canton, which ironically was also full of tough Irish immigrants.'

'Aye, I know Canton well, good pubs there... nice old Victorian houses. And you've been here ever since?'

'Well yes and no I suppose. After leaving technical college I'd often travel back to London. I picked up with a few of my old school friends. We used to enjoy hanging out down the West End.'

What Charley failed to let on was that socialising in north London she soon became aware of, and got pretty close to, a good number of hard men there too.

I asked if she ever wanted to go back to London to

live but she always seemed to change the subject. Said she had too many bad memories, knew too many dodgy people. She'd tell me a few stories of scraps in the clubs, said the bouncers were really mean, much meaner than me and it was a different world. Bright lights, fast cars and faster women. Quick justice if you ever stepped out of line.

'You'd never survive,' she joked.

'Really? You an expert on my line of work all of a sudden?' I replied.

I was intrigued by her tales though. Captivated by my own sanguine view of this big city world I really did know nothing about. I wanted to know more though and thinking about what my dad had said about leaving Wales knew that one day I would definitely head up there too.

We were blissfully happy for six months, we spent a wonderful Christmas together. I was becoming quite domesticated and even allowed her to pick out a few items of fashionable clothes for me. It was just as well as I would often go out wearing a string vest and tight jeans when it was snowing – just to show off my muscles. I didn't have a clue and didn't care as long as you could see my seventeen-inch arms. "Curls for girls" as the rugby boys used to say back in the day.

Then I came home early one night. I was doing the odd night in a small, basement club down Charles Street. It was quiet so we shut up shop and fucked off. I sneaked into our house in case Charley was asleep, not wanting to wake up my beautiful bird.

I crept silently upstairs but froze when I heard her sobbing. Terrible tears, really breaking her heart she was. I hated to see her upset but hung back on the landing, outside the bedroom door.

'I can't.'

A pause on the other end of the line.

'Not happening, I want to keep...'

More silence.

'Nobody. Just a local lad. No, you'll leave him out of this...'

Quiet.

'Yes, alright, I will. If you promise.'

I hear the phone put back on the receiver.

Quietly backtracking, I descend the stairs and open and close the front door with a bang. I jog back up the staircase.

'Hi love, everything okay?'

Charley has wiped her face but I can still see her eyes are red. Her tanned skin has gone birch-bark white. She looks ill and jumps up to head for the bathroom.

When she emerges, a few minutes later, she smiles at me and opens her arms. Accepting the invitation I walk slowly towards her and cwtch her close.

'I was thinking about my dad,' she confesses. 'I'm alright. Have to be eh?'

I kiss the top of her head then unbutton my shirt. I pull away, remove my shoes and socks followed by my black trousers. We slip between the sheets and hold each other close again for a few minutes before she takes the lead and reaches down with her right hand to caress my thighs.

It doesn't take me many seconds before I'm wanting her so badly. We kiss passionately and I sense urgency in my lover's body. Her perfume smells of coffee and vanilla. It heightens my senses as I feel her silky, warm skin press ever closer.

'Oh Paul,' she whispers, and with a sudden aching clarity I knew I must have her now. My hands move up and down the perfect contours of her body as she turns her face up to look at me. Her lips tremble as I feel her hot breath upon my mouth. I softly touch her neck, her shoulders and become acutely aware of the surge of her breasts, the curvature of her buttocks.

The inside of the room is faintly lit by the moonlight outside the window and somewhere on the street we hear the screeching of a car before deathly silence again. All I can hear now is the loud beating of our hearts.

I'm hot and pull the bedclothes back as I support myself on my powerful arms. I stare down at Charley's exquisite form and am mesmerised by her tender movements. I watch in wonder as her perfectly rounded breasts rise and fall with each breath and marvel as each nipple darkens and hardens in the cool air of our bedroom. Charley quickly pulls me down on top of her. Our breath coming in gasps.

Longing… hunger… greed.

*

It was that time of year when the daffodils started sprouting all along the castle wall and the days were getting lighter and longer. It should have been a time to think ahead, plan for the future even. I'd never been so content in all my miserable life.

Then Charley left. No reason, no note. She just upped and went. It was 1987 and I was utterly distraught.

At first I supposed she was visiting friends and had forgotten to leave a note. Then my mind started to play tricks. Invent things. Maybe she was seeing someone else? I most likely frightened half the male population of the city staring daggers at them and wondering if that was the bastard. I even toyed with the idea that maybe she'd been kidnapped. Even considered going to the pigs before it finally dawned on me.

There was no secret, no magic formula I'd misread. She'd gone because she didn't want to be with me anymore. As simple as that. We were just too different. She was so much more street-wise than me and being older she wanted someone to provide for her. Someone she could depend on. Someone that was definitely coming home every night. You might as well have flipped a coin in my shadowy world.

I replayed scenes, rewound conversations and went over and over things from our last month together. Eventually I convinced myself I'd found the answers, hidden away somewhere in her words, oblivious to the real reason.

All of a sudden I understood. All her life she'd had to fight to survive, to rely on her wits. She needed someone more mature. I was just too much of a kid for her. I was too young to settle down and start behaving like a real man so she just buggered off.

I cried until June.

Six

In those early days, after Charley had first gone AWOL, I spent hours slouched on my pillows, half awake, half asleep. I'd sit in my bedroom alone, drinking strong lager and listening to Velvet Underground and Doors albums until I took the edge off. I'd stare out the window at the people passing by. I'd fixate on a raindrop, follow as it slowly ran down the glass, then look back up and watch another do the same. I was in a world of pain and darkness. I floated in and out of limbo and I wandered for miles all over the compact city that would leave a permanent scar on me.

During these mostly directionless ambles around the cold city streets, I'd occasionally stop and pause to look up at the towering buildings. I knew what it took to build these huge structures but didn't see the point of them. Hotels yes but office blocks? What were all those people doing inside? Typing away, passing pieces of paper to and fro. They were wasting their lives. They didn't make anything of use to anyone. I didn't get it.

I was also in a constant state of panic that occasionally turned to rage. Anger that someone had shattered my life so badly without a care in the world. I'd repeatedly ask the same questions to the gods of heartache and loss. I never got an answer that made sense and the hollow sensation in the pit of my stomach never left me.

Eventually I'd end up near a café or bread shop where I'd quickly snap out of my trance and buy a pasty or a bacon roll. I washed it down with a Lucozade.

In the afternoons I sometimes popped in to the pub. I usually stayed local, one of the Brains inns down the bay - the White Hart, the Ship or the Packet. I'd sit harbouring a pint at the bar and turn around every time the door creaked. My pulse would jump whenever I saw a flash of blonde hair. At night it was worse though.

If I wasn't working I often went to a club; so I could prolong the time before I had to return home to an empty house. I saw my world from the other side. Packed tight with sweating bodies, the heavy bass beat barely changing as one so-called song merged into another in a non-stop noise that thumped through your chest. Women danced around bags thrown on the floor, men lurched on bars and small ledges, cradling their bottles of lager and trying to look cool so a girl might choose them. I usually just had a few beers then went home. Even in my confused state I knew I shouldn't get too drunk, just in case someone recognised me and fancied their chances.

In work I took it out on my customers. I never actually considered myself a big lad although I knew I wasn't exactly small. Not that size is as important as you might assume in my racket. Presence yes, but most of the nasty bastards I encountered were tiny. And the smaller they were the more likely they were to be carrying a blade, which everyone could do without.

There was one particular evil prick I came upon around that time. He was about five foot nothing, slightly built, but straight away I knew he was nuts. You could see it in his dead, grey eyes. I learnt later he was a well-known member of the Soul Crew, Cardiff City's hooligan football firm, and had been arrested about twenty times before. It was this fact that helped me convince the police on two separate occasions that me putting him in hospital was simply self-defence.

The first time he just took a swing at me, for no apparent reason, in the men's bogs of Coco's, the club I was working at. I took the punch on the cheek and instinctively hit back, with interest. His lip split and blood gushed down his chin. I thought he'd take the hint but he just scowled at me. It was then I saw his hand go to his jacket pocket. I knew he wasn't going for his handkerchief.

Out came the steel and now it was serious. I didn't hesitate. I rushed at him, leapt off the floor and kicked him in the chest, my size thirteen boot catching him full on in the sternum. He flew across the toilet floor and crashed into the bosch. His head smashed on the porcelain sink and blood poured from a head wound. I asked a few punters to go get backup for me, in case he had any friends who wanted a bit too, then quickly picked up the kitchen knife and waited for Nick, John H, big Rob or one of the other lads to turn up.

The second occasion I was stood on the door of a different late-night watering hole, on my own again, when I spied a small figure slowly skulking along the wall next to the club entrance. I didn't realise it was the same guy until he got really close and lunged at me with a Samurai sword waving like a windmill above his head.

I hated knifes. I'd sustained a nasty slash on my forearm in my first month working doors in Cardiff but this was undeniably grim. Luckily I was sober and had slightly faster reflexes than my attacker. Ducking to the right I felt the deadly weapon swish the air just inches from my skull as it clanged on the brick wall behind me.

Again I reacted automatically, not really thinking about my own safety. I rushed at the madman, knocking him over with a shoulder to the face and stared through wide pupils as he tumbled backwards into the street. I knew I had to get that weapon away from him so I jumped down the front step and landed on his right hand, which still gripped the blade.

He screamed out something unkind about my parentage as I stamped on his hand a second time. I was not taking any chances – he was going down big time.

In fairness a few lads waiting to be let inside the club had rushed inside to fetch the other bouncers. If they hadn't I might have gone down for murder. I was kicking the little fucker in the face, in the bollocks, in the ribs, in a frenzy now, but just before I jumped onto his head a few of the other doormen grabbed hold of me. Soothing words helped calm me down a little and they managed to pull me out of harms way before my foot crushed the life out of the horrible twat.

The Old Bill were quite understanding and clearly pleased to acquire the nutter's decorative sword for their latest TV appeal for a knife amnesty in the city. I decided there and then twenty-five quid a night wasn't enough for this shit.

*

I'd gotten a bit reckless after Charley left. Didn't really care if I got glassed or beaten up. I'd put up a mental wall but to be honest it was tiring. I also took it out on punters who perhaps, in hindsight, didn't deserve it.

In the past I'd never been particularly bothered about tapping off with the girls who threw themselves at us bouncers. I could take it or leave it. But around that time I did start to take anyone remotely interested in me back to my gaff. I wasn't interested in them as human beings and usually kicked them out in the morning without even offering them a cup of tea. It's easy to become brutalised, dehumanised even, living in that twilight realm. Soon enough though I woke up and realised a change of scenery was needed. Before I ended up seriously injured myself, or maybe even killing someone.

Most of the bouncers I knew in Cardiff at that time were generally nice guys. The odd couple were cocks but on the whole the majority of the blokes were just trying to get by. To get through the night without getting hurt was the only mantra. Plenty of boys liked a scrap for sure but most had just ended up doing the job because they fell into it – a mate asked them, the pub was short staffed and so on. It was also a very unpredictable scene. Work one month, nothing the next. Clubs opened and clubs closed. Eventually you got to know the faces though, the good guys. The ones you could depend on in times of crisis. I liked those guys.

*

'Fuck it. I'm off to London,' I announced out loud.

'Where's that?' said the valley slapper who for some reason was eating my cornflakes.

I just stared for a minute. Her complete ignorance of the world even more limited than mine.

'It's in England love.'

'Ah yeh, where those slimy politicians live, I know. In that big old house, I seen it on the telly mun. Wha da ya wanna go there for butt?'

'Why not?' I mumble in reply but not really interested in intellectual conversation with Marilyn's Welsh love child.

'Nah mun. There's all sorts of funny people up there, all foreign like, ragheads smelling of curry, black uns too, and all them posh ones, everythin', nah, you'll be better stayin' 'ere mun,' my well-informed, self-appointed travel consultant helpfully pointed out.

Looking across the breakfast bar I noticed she had mascara smudged across her cheeks and her chubby, bloated tits were barely back in her dress. She wasn't bad looking and she'd been extremely enthusiastic to demonstrate her gymnastic prowess last night but it was obvious that her path lay on a different course to mine. She liked the valleys – the inexorable consistency, and couldn't wait to get back.

While I lived in Cardiff, I was still in Wales and the valley folk loved to party in the city. Every weekend I had a stark reminder of where I came from and what life was like there. Although it was extremely unfair of me I'd begun to despise them for keeping me shackled here so long.

'Time to go love. Don't forget your knickers will you?'

'Oh you fuckin' romantic you,' came the reply,

before she changed tack and quickly shot a smile my way. 'Not up for round two are we love?'

'Nah sorry, have to pass on that one beautiful, you sucked all the goodness out of me last night.'

Although she poked her tongue out at me I knew she was still happy as she now had a great story to relate to everyone back home. One that would no doubt move her up the social rankings of popularity and street cred in her local pub on Beaufort Street.

I finished packing my rucksack about ten minutes after I slammed the front door behind her. My only thought was whether I walked to the station right there and then or chickened out and waited until Monday morning.

In actual fact I was most likely sat on the train, London bound, before Sharon had found her way to the bus stop to scan the timetable for the X4 back to Brynmawr.

Seven

1988

Paddington station was like a zoo. People rushing around in every direction like crazy. Where were they all going in such a hurry? I seemed to be the only one who was moving slowly. I was walking along the platform trying to work out how to get to the tube when I saw a comely Chinese woman.

'Excuse me love, how do I get to Soho?'

I got a blank look from the frightened tourist who completely ignored me before scurrying off. Better choose the next one more carefully.

Asking the same question again I instinctively knew this stunning lass wouldn't be so rude.

'Bright lights is it Taffy?' she beamed.

'No, I've got an address to stay,' I answered sheepishly.

'Ah, alright then. Oxford Circus would be your best bet,' she paused as her eyes roved all over me. 'Or you could try Piccadilly and walk, you good-looking devil you.'

'Thanks very much.'

The brunette beauty unashamedly ran her eyes up and down my body again then added.

'If you want a tour guide you only have to ask lovely.'

Although slightly out of my comfort zone her warm smile and familiar accent immediately brought back happy memories. Classical conditioning is a wonderful thing.

'That's very kind but I just need to get to my

mate's place.'

She wasn't giving up easily though. 'Soho you say? Mmm. Think it was Henry VIII who started all that. Created a royal park there in 1536.'

'Really? I didn't know.'

'Yeh, I'm a mind of useless information me old China. And all free to the right customer.'

'Okay, thanks, I better be going though,' I hesitated.

'Suit yourself... but if you change your mind give us a call.'

She handed me a piece of paper with the word Millie and a 01 phone number scrawled, almost indecipherable, below it.

I was still smirking by the time I got off at Piccadilly Circus and walked the rest of the way. It took me another hour to find my way to the Soho address that Brad, one of the English doormen from Cardiff, had given me months before. I didn't know which tube train line to get on and ended up going back and forth the wrong way a couple of times before I eventually worked out I wanted the brown, Bakerloo line. I learnt quickly though after that.

Although Soho had a bad reputation as a base for the sex industry, by the late 80s the area had undergone a certain gentrification. Upmarket restaurants and film and media companies had moved in and setup shop alongside the few remnants of the old sex venues that remained. A big gay community also appeared to be growing in Soho at this time.

The address I had was for The Ship on Wardour Street. I asked behind the bar if they had rooms to rent and was told in no uncertain terms, no.

'Brad sent me,' I tried.

It had the desired effect.

'Ah yeh man, no problem,' said the Rasta pulling me a pint of best bitter. 'How is Brad?'

'Not bad,' I replied. 'We used to work together in Cardiff.'

'Ah yeh man, I heard he was out in the sticks. That in Wales yeh?'

'Aye, somewhere near there,' I confirmed.

Eight

It took me about two nights wandering between clubs and being introduced to various friends of friends before I got my first job in London. To be fair there were so many clubs and bars that needed bouncers I could have found a decent gig myself but as Brad had such a good reputation as a doorman I thought it best if I used my association with him to best effect. I figured I could always suss out a better job later on if need be.

The diverse history of the Soho streets became my introduction to the city's nightlife. I found it astonishing. From the gangs of organised crime on Gerard Street, to swinging London and Carnaby Street. The artists of Dean Street, the trials of Oscar Wilde for being gay and the Stones for being junkies - it was all here. Karl Marx had laid out the Communist manifesto in a pub on Great Windmill Street while musicians, poets and writers inhabited the rest. It was so different to the valleys. Sure we had history aplenty but this was a far more sophisticated, all-encompassing education. Just being there at that time introduced me to a living breathing account of how the whole, modern world had emerged from ancient times.

Unlike Cardiff though the London scene was not merely huge, especially considering the size of the city and the myriad of boroughs and different areas, but it was also very changeable. Clubs and live music venues were everywhere but things constantly evolved.

It was all a bit mystical at that time too. The only

way you found out what was cool was by hanging out in a particular record shop or around the Kensington market area. One month I was mingling with emaciated students as they listened to prog rock group Marillion at the Marquee and then I was camping it up in the new Madame JoJo's. Not that I could ever claim to be particularly feminine.

*

I was working most evenings now as well, in a few different clubs scattered around the north of London. Most nights were calm. I got into a few scuffles, usually with gangs of boys too drunk to behave properly but I was much more easy-going in them days, having slowly got my head back in the right place.

Sometimes after throwing certain people out I'd tell the lads to go sober up for half an hour, behave themselves and I'd let them back in. If they were polite and apologetic I'd be fine. What always attracts a bouncer's attention is when boys behave in a certain way – unpredictable, over-excited, loud or aggressive. Then they have no chance of being let in.

You'd think it was fairly obvious to punters but drink in, sense out. Gangs of boys are also welcome as long as they are tidy. What doormen don't like is a gang of knobheads, or even just the one!

Sometimes I'd use a bit of diplomacy if I didn't like the look of someone. I'd tell them we'd made a mistake by letting in too many boys and that there were so many in the club now that you'd be hard pressed to find any birds. Most lads only want to come into a club full of girls so it usually worked.

A few of the other bouncers would hit the dance floor. It was a good way to keep tabs on everyone and made us look more human to the customers but I was never much of a dancer. The conformist valleys saw to that. None of the boys danced when I was growing up. If they did, the other lads called them gay or something equally disparaging and we'd only make it onto the shiny parquet at the end of the night when the beer had well and truly taken its toll, the slow songs started and we were desperate to cop off.

*

By the end of the year I was getting to know my way around much of the vast, sprawling capital city and even managed a few shifts at Shoom, the club that effectively kicked off the acid-house craze in London. Originally in Southwark, the club soon moved to a larger YMCA basement on Tottenham Court Road.

I suppose for me that is when the clubs really changed. Drugs, drugs and more drugs. Sure they were around before that time but the new dance clubs were really just drug clubs. Instead of alcohol for kicks kids were turning to tablets. And where drugs went so did money. Big money. And where big money was to be found, so were the nasty cunts.

It was about this time that I met Patrick.

Nine

1989

In Cardiff I might have been a reasonably tough guy but I was still nowhere near the hardest. Yeh I was big and imposing, but with copious amounts of steroids, the training aid of choice back then, who wasn't. Most of the clubs there knew who I was and I later learnt I had a fair reputation, especially as everyone on the circuit also seemed to know I didn't *do roids* and that my muscles were all natural, honed from genetics, the gym and hard work. It was also common knowledge I hated drugs.

In the much bigger city of London though, I was a nobody. Just another face from the suburbs that no-one knew or cared about. Reputation was everything here. It had to be, otherwise some very nasty scraps might have taken place if you didn't know when to back down and when to fight. It wasn't that you couldn't beat the crap out of the guy mouthing off two inches from your face but if his boss was bigger than your boss... you let him win or at least think he'd won.

'Paul is it?' said Patrick, sizing me up as he spoke.

'Yes sir,' I knew when to be polite too.

'Heard good things about you boyo.'

'Thank you, mister...'

His gnarled raised hand stopped me mid-sentence.

'I'm looking for a new lad who can handle himself. One of my boys got greedy and had to be let go. The Thames is exceptionally cold this time of year too.'

'You'll be doing mostly driving to start with. Michael here will show you the ropes. You interested?'

Michael was a short, stocky lad, about thirty years old with a flat nose. I noticed his hard shape through the cheap suit he wore and knew instinctively he could handle himself. He wasn't frightened of me one bit and stood behind Patrick, just off to the side, wholly relaxed.

The boss held out his huge hand. He wasn't exactly a big man but his hands were massive. About forty years old, he had piercing olive-green eyes, thinning hair, slightly orange at the sides but perhaps more sandy on top. He wore a black suit, great cut and instantly recognisable as expensive, tailored. Shiny black shoes, possibly Italian, jutted out from beetle-black trousers. A gold Omega watch and a gold sovereign ring completed the look.

When he looked at you he looked deep into you. Searching for weakness or subservience – I was never quite sure which.

I had a choice to make and had to make it quick. I could shake his hand, earn a fortune but be forever tied to this vicious gangster's crew or politely decline and then crawl back to the quietest, most insignificant club I could find to work at, or better still simply leave London for good and go home with my tail between my legs.

If I'd known then what I know now, and also what was to happen a few years later I would have said, 'Thank you for your exceedingly kind offer sir but I'm afraid I'm going to have to decline. My bed-ridden granny wants me to take her hang-gliding back home in Tonypandy.'

Unfortunately, in those days I was still a bit naïve

and also a bit of a mental case. I craved excitement, even if it might end up getting me killed. Bollocks to it. What did I have to lose?

I shook the Irishman's hand.

I found the restaurant easily enough. It was a nice looking place, flowers in baskets were hanging up outside, a few chairs and tables on the pavement. Very classy, new furnishings set amongst a much older wood interior. Michael decided to stay in the car.

I walked in, casually asked for Reg and waited. On reflection I should have signalled for Michael to join me when instead of Reg the owner, two large, thickset Micks with pink noses and wild red hair appeared with baseball bats.

'Hey lads, calm down. I'm only collecting,' I attempted to pacify the situation.

'Well collect this then you Taffy bastard,' as the first swing nearly took my head off.

Luckily I'd seen it coming and ducked just in time. I wasn't so lucky with the second lad. He'd jabbed his weapon forward like a sword, catching me full on in the stomach and winding me.

Never being one to take a step back I quickly unbent my frame and lunged forward grabbing Tweedle-Dum by the throat and swinging him around by his collar before letting go and using his own considerable momentum to throw him across the room.

His tag partner d'Artagnan had by now landed a

second blow across my back but although it hurt like hell I was now in for a penny and there was only one thing on my mind – kill this fuckin' ginger man-mountain.

Before he could strike the bat again I slapped him hard around the left ear with a huge haymaker and while he was disorientated for a few seconds punched up under his throat with my left fist. I heard a snap as his Adam's apple cracked. I silently thanked my old mate Nick for that move.

One down, one to go.

I turned quickly, just in time to see the first man get back to his feet and start running towards me. Big mistake in this open room. Like a champion matador I casually stepped aside and grabbed the weapon from his hands as he passed. I didn't wait for an invitation to do a Don Bradman on his two testicles. I just hit them for six.

His high-pitched scream or maybe it was the noise of breaking wood woke Michael from his daydream and he sprinted from the car to lend a hand.

'Took your fuckin' time,' I scolded.

'Sorry Paul, I was listening to the footie scores on the radio. What the fuck happened, this should have been easy?'

'Okay, but what do we do now though?'

'I dunno. They've never not paid before. Best we get out of here, Patrick's not going to like this though.'

*

He didn't. After Michael had given his version I gave mine. They were close enough for him to believe us and within an hour we were back there with ten lads smashing the restaurant to bits.

After the demolition job, Reg, the now slightly-bruised owner, was sheepishly plonked in a chair and shaking like a leaf. Patrick got out of the Daimler that was parked outside and walked in.

It was then I discovered what a nasty piece of work really looked like. One of the gang produced a hammer and chisel and poor Reg, who I suppose was only trying to keep more of his business takings, learnt the hard way what happened when you crossed one of the up and coming crime bosses of north London.

We never had a problem collecting money from that eatery or any other place from the same patch again. And after the impromptu DIY lesson I'd witnessed, first hand as it were, we never set eyes on pathetic Reg again either. He was no doubt hiding in the back of the diner and praying he'd added up the money properly. Not that I imagine he ever did much licking of his fingers while counting the notes out.

Ten

I only popped in on my night off. Thought I'd get a quick bite to eat and a bottle or two of lager to wash it down. The pub was about a quarter full, nothing much going on so I take a corner table and order from the dog-eared bar menu. Rachel the dark-haired, ghost-faced, pixie-pretty little waitress brings me a beer and I pay for the meal and one more drink. I then put the same amount down on top as a tip and give her a wink.

'Oh thank you Paul darlin', you don't have to though.'

'Ah, your smile alone is worth it.' I imagine her cringing as she turns away, instantly realising I'm still not particularly cool with the ladies.

After draining the first lager I nod to the bar for the next. It's quiet, a Tuesday evening and one of our pubs so there shouldn't be any hassle. How wrong can someone be?

I'm still happily munching on my burger when a chair crashes through the front window. I look up to see a gang of about eight skinheads heading my way. I knew there was a back exit to the place but as the staff were always so nice to me, not to mention the fact I really liked them, I stayed.

By the time reinforcements arrived I was half dead. The thick pile of floral carpet was soaking up my blood and my face was not as pretty as it once was but I'd survive. Apparently I'd acquitted myself fairly well, taking out about five of their crowd before succumbing to their blows. Luckily for me it was only a good beating I took. I found out later they had knives, bats and metal bars with them but had left them in the vans. They wrongly assumed that because they could only see a few customers inside, just regular punters, that they wouldn't need them. I suppose I'd always been lucky like that.

*

Michael brought me a massive bag of grapes, as a joke.

'Thought I'd come to cheer you up ya daft bastard. You should have run.'

'Don't make me laugh, it hurts everywhere.'

'Aye, how's the head then Taff? They say you took a right hammering.'

'I'll live. What you doing here anyway? Hunting nurses now is it mate?'

'Na, just come to give you the good news.'

The pain came in layers. I'd think it was over then a new wave would hit me. I was on medication but it wore off through the night and I had to wait until the morning shift before I got any more.

'Michael, my tongue is so swollen it fills my mouth, which is like an Arab's dap...'

'Ah, so that's it. Thought you were auditioning for what's my lisp.'

'And if my knuckles didn't throb so bad I'd belt you...'

'Mmm.'

'Hang on, what's wrong with my head?' his earlier comment gradually registering.

'Well, face essentially,' said Michael.

'Oh dear, is it bad?'

'Well let's just say you have a bruise the size of a football. You look like petrol in a puddle boyo.'

'Wonderful. What was the good news then?'

'Well, Patrick heard how you reacted. He was well impressed. The staff were grateful too, especially the cute emo bird who works there…'

'Aye? Knew my huge tip would pay dividends,' I tried to laugh but couldn't. My ribs didn't want to let me.

'Anyway, he's decided you should be rewarded with a special job when you get out of hospital. He sends his best…'

'Marvellous.'

'Hey, take the praise when you can, doesn't happen often. He says take it easy, rest up, get your strength back and he'll sort you out a bit of cash too.'

'Okay mate, ta. Who were they anyhow?'

'Yep, right there, past tense is correct.'

'Shit, what happened?'

'A classic turf war affair, you know. One firm smashes up your pub, a few days later you smash up theirs. A bit childish if you ask me, why the idiots can't stick to football matches I'll never know.'

*

Michael told me I didn't want to know so I asked a few of the other lads what happened to the rival gang who'd beaten me up. It didn't make pleasant listening. After a brief shootout their boss was dead, although the boys didn't think he was actually dead when Patrick turned up.

By the time his head had been removed from his body with a chainsaw though...

I also learnt his teeth were pulled out and his hands chopped off, to impede identification, in case the police ever found the rest of him. I don't think they ever did although to be fair disposing of a body is not as easy as people might first believe.

One of the most notorious methods employed by Chicago gangsters during the prohibition era was to tie chains around a corpse or bury a victim in concrete before throwing them in the sea or a river. However this method isn't full proof as escaping gases from a decaying body have even been known to crack concrete and then the body will float back to the surface. Having said that I think they sunk what was left of this unfortunate chap in a large lake north of the city. He's probably still there, unless the fish have eaten him like in the movies.

*

When I got discharged from the lovely little nurses' expert care I still ached all over. Bone deep pains. I was grateful for the new job though. It would take me another month to recover properly so it would be good to ease myself back in gently.

I even bought a suit, three Van Heusen shirts and a couple of ties to rotate each day. She liked her men to look the part I was told.

My new work was going to be good for me. It would get me away from the nitty-gritty, the violence at the sharp end. I had a good feeling about this.

At twenty-seven I was still comparatively young and impressionable but not completely dehumanized. I was still capable of empathy, I never really wanted to hurt anyone, not unless they asked for it of course, and above all I still craved and believed in true romance.

As well as my battered body the last few years of work had without doubt taken their toll on my patchy love life. I'd had a few brief affairs, seen one girl for about two months but that ended the same way as all the rest – I got bored, she got bored and then one of us just left.

In 1989 all that changed.

Eleven

It was Friday afternoon and things were quiet. We were sat in the backroom of an old pub on Canonbury Place. I loved the old boozers in London, especially the quiet ones tucked away down little alleys. They had so much character and I often wondered what great stories the walls could tell, although with Michael around I rarely needed a history book as he seemed to know everything vaguely interesting about the city.

True to form Michael informed me that this one was nearly three hundred years old and George Orwell had written his most famous novel, 1984, in the beer garden. I didn't believe him at first 'cos he was always telling me porkies but it turns out he was telling the truth this time.

A light wind was blowing in off the Thames. It thread its way through the maze of streets before seeping way down into your bones. The sun was dipping in and out from behind big fluffy clouds, splashing light on the historic buildings of the greatest city in the world. I was grateful to be inside, in the warm.

The Jameson's was poured and small glasses passed around the table.

'Okay, so the boss is away for a bit. If anyone asks he's on holiday,' said Frank, number two to Patrick.

'Yes boss,' Michael and I replied in unison.

Frank was older than Patrick. His dyed black hair betrayed by the silver bristles that were sprinkled all over his pink-pale cheeks. His thin mouth was set in a perpetual sneer. He was overweight and had a loose flabby neck. He didn't look the healthiest specimen but underestimate him at your own risk. He'd been there at the start, a father-like figure when Patrick was being groomed for better things as a teenager in the early seventies. When he spoke you listened, mainly because no-one ever wanted to ask him to repeat himself.

He used to drive the vans that I'd heard about. When people went missing, permanently.

'So, in the meantime you two have been tasked with looking after her ladyship. I obviously don't need to tell you not to fuck this up or upset her in any way. You drive her wherever she wants to go, you wait for her to get her hair done, buy some poxy dresses or whatever feckin' nonsense birds do these days, then you drive her back home safely, simples.'

'Yes boss,' we harmonised like a stuck record.

'Should be an easy job and we're not expecting any distress on this one as all's quiet on the western front at the moment.'

'Yes boss.'

Frank knocked his whiskey back and indicated for us to do the same.

'Start Monday, Patrick's house right, ten o'clock sharp. Not that she gets up very early, the dozy fuckin' bitch.'

'Okay Frank,' I smirked.

'Well fuck off then. Enjoy the weekend.'

Twelve

We all knew Patrick was visiting the states of course, trying to clinch a big deal now that he was allowing drugs to be sold through his clubs. He wasn't backwards coming forwards and recognised the potential his outlets offered. His trip also gave me and Michael a bit of breathing space.

We decided we should let our hair down. That weekend the two of us went to a couple of pubs in Whitechapel. Although Michael sometimes came across a bit slow to the other lads I knew it was all an act. He was actually a very switched on bloke who knew loads of stuff about the history of gangs, especially in London.

We found a quiet-ish spot in the corner of the boozer and had a good chat.

'So are we moving into the narcotics industry now then?' I asked Michael.

'Aye, looks like boyo.'

'You comfortable with that?' I enquired.

'I don't get to feckin' choose now do I? And neither do you.'

'Suppose not,' I resigned myself. 'I thought that with all the cash from the clubs, bit of protection, the odd bit of this and that…'

'First up Paul mate, don't think. It can be extremely hazardous to your health.'

'Well, isn't Patrick doing great. He must be worth a small fortune?' I asked.

'Yeh, but like all of his kind he wants to be bigger, richer, you know. Stand still in this game and your dog meat.'

'Guess so. Just thought he had enough like.'

'Okay Einstein, how much is enough exactly?'

'Alright, I get it mate,' I said.

'Trust me, he is not ever going to be happy. He wants it all and won't stop until he gets it or someone stops him getting it.'

Michael then proceeded to give me a brief précis of the modern criminal underworld. The dangerous world I'd been dragged into a touch too fast for my liking.

'Okay, listen. Back in the fifties it was safes right.'

'Blowing safes?'

'Aye, pissed off blokes, back after the war and out of work but highly skilled with explosives. So what do they do? They start cracking safes.'

'Makes sense.'

'Right. But they cottoned on to that. Designed better safes and it took too long to break into them.'

'So what happened after that?' I asked.

'Next was wages runs. Everything was done in cash in the sixties. Hundreds of blokes working on a building site got paid every week in pound notes...'

'I worked on site, yeh all cash,' I interrupted.

'Aye, well it didn't take the boys long to work out who was driving the Ford Escort through the gates of the site on a Thursday afternoon. It was the same for factories and even offices.'

'So you just grabbed the bags of cash?'

'Be rude not to boyo.'

'Didn't they have protection? A couple of guys like us?'

'Nah, crazy eh?' chuckled Michael. 'Eventually though they started using armoured cars so that little caper was off the menu as well.'

'So, what you're really saying is that crime is merely a game. An intelligence game, survival of the fittest and so on. The crooks take the easy money until the good guys fight back or change their ways.'

'To be sure Paul, you're dead right there. Apart from one thing.'

'What's that?'

'We are the good guys.' He laughed out loud.

'Okay, so what was next?'

'Banks.'

'Ah of course, always wanted to rob a bank. Used to plan it in my head as a kid.'

'Yeh, they were easy as hell, so the old guys told me. No security, not even cameras in the early days. I don't remember it of course, before my time, but apparently they used to have large wooden boxes, full of cash, just sitting on the desks. Imagine the temptation!'

'Alright, so that's when sawn-off shotguns made an appearance right?'

'Yeh, spot on. Of course the police started to fight back as soon as the guns appeared. The Sweeney shot to fame in the seventies as well. Bigger crooks than the blaggers my dad always said.'

'Okay, so what about now, the eighties?' I asked, eager to know what it was I might be expected to do next.

'Hold your horses boyo. I'm on a roll now...'

'Aye, I can tell. University fuckin' Challenge you'll be on next, specialist subject, "How to knock off a

Barclays".'

'That's Mastermind you dick.'

'Oh yeh, sorry. Carry on Magnus O'Reilly,' I grinned.

'Right. After the banks wised up to the gangs it was security vans. You know, Securicor stuff.'

'Ah yeh, I've heard about that, pavement artists right!'

'Yep, that's right. I've done a few myself,' added Michael.

'Really?'

'Oh aye, hell of a rush!'

'Come on, what's now?' I pleaded.

'Well I guess since eighty three everyone's been looking for that big score.'

'Brinks Mat you mean yeh?'

'Yeh, Patrick was always on the lookout for something like that, but now I reckon he's gonna be moving us into drugs full time.'

'Oh great. Shit. I fuckin' hate drugs.'

'Aye, so I've heard boyo. Well get used to them is all I can advise. They are not going away.'

*

We drank up and grabbed a taxi. The black cab soon took us across Tower Bridge and south of the river where we headed to The Fridge in Brixton. It was a big party pub, popular with the new romantics and had regulars like Boy George and Soul II Soul. It was a bit too gay for me, being the straight valley boy I was but Michael found it fascinating. Not that he was queer or anything – he just used to think they were hilarious.

Although it wasn't our patch we were still recognised because of who we worked for. That was the thing with clubs. Most people think you'd want to stop the tough guys coming in but certain people, like us at that time, could be seen as an asset to a place.

Instead of causing trouble the opposite is true. A well-known or successful firm that decides to patronise your club or use it as a base can actually keep it calm. If the owner of a club has a tidy little crew in residence then no-one else is going to cause hassle. In fact other punters will start to come to the place just to see or be seen with the faces. You became part of the in-crowd as Bryan Ferry would have said.

*

Most nights in the city blurred into one. But this particular Friday I do remember very vividly. It was because it was the last time I went with a girl from London town.

At first I thought she was a bloke, a tranny or something. Heidi was brown like gingerbread, six-foot two tall and in high heels she was eyeball to eyeball with me. Lean as a rake with huge afro hair you would have been forgiven for thinking she belonged in seventies New York. As I got closer I was picturing what an Olympic high jumper looked like.

Back in my digs she became a tigress though, tearing my shirt off, the buttons popping apart before I had time to undo them. Her breathing was rapid, her pupils dilated and her skin on fire. I never asked if she was alright. I was too busy squashing the life out of her athletic frame with my seventeen stone of hard muscle. She didn't complain.

Saturday was wasted by the time we'd finished round three or four and I offered to buy her breakfast in a café I knew in Stockwell.

'It's half past four love. In the afternoon,' she giggled. 'Don't you ever get tired?'

I dipped my head in acknowledgement. 'I'm hungry,' was all I could mumble.

'Me too. Do they do pancakes with syrup?' she laughed as she spoke and her eyes twinkled with mischief.

*

We headed north, crossed back over the Thames and drank in a few pubs on our way to Tottenham Court Road, which had become a favourite spot of mine.

After a bite to eat Heidi dragged me back towards Hackney where she took me to the Four Aces club in Dalston.

Founded in the sixties, the club was one of the first to introduce black music to London and in its heyday was visited by Mick Jagger, Debbie Harry, Bob Dylan, Marc Bolan and The Clash.

Although it wasn't exactly legal at the time we got in alright, and I watched in awe as an acid house party spun around my un-drugged head. It was another wild night where my black beauty visited the toilets far too often for my liking but she was so sexy I put up with it.

Most of Sunday was spent in the bath or my bed. I reluctantly said goodbye to Heidi late that night as I had to get up early for the boss's boring babysitting job. I was feeling heavy-lidded and light-headed. Possibly lack of sugar and sleep.

'Ring me babe?' Heidi tossed me a slip of paper with her telephone number scribbled on it.

'Yeh definitely,' I smirked, already thinking about when I'd see her again and what other kinky stuff we might get up to.

I stuck the telly on and watched the news. I wanted to see if the world had stopped spinning while I was shagging myself stupid for nearly three days.

Thinking about Heidi made me realise old wounds were slowly healing and maybe there was light at the end of the tunnel. Yeh, things are looking up.

I fell back into my armchair and listened to a story about the collapse of the Berlin Wall and how difficult it was going to be for Germany to assimilate a whole, bankrupt country into the west. I open my eyes as a glass of water slips from my hand and spills on the carpet. I get up, press the switch on the wall and go to bed. Falling into a deep sleep I have a lovely dream about caramel-coloured thighs wrapped around my open mouth.

I never did ring Heidi though. Something major and unexpected came up instead.

Thirteen

Slumped sideways on my bed, feet hanging over the edge I'm floating in and out of sleep. Drifting between pornographic dreams of a pecan-brown Nubian princess and walks on the beach back in south Wales. My mind was racing. Something wasn't right. A sixth sense was trying to tell me something important but I couldn't put my finger on it.

Monday morning. I woke up reasonably early. I could see out the window from my bed – the sky was unblemished with neither cloud nor smog. Ultramarine in colour. It was a beautiful day.

I jumped out of bed with a headache pulsing. I did fifty fast press-ups, followed by fifty sit-ups. Repeating the exercises, I did the second set slowly, on purpose. Then I grabbed two twenty-kilogram dumbbells and did a few sets of curls and shoulder presses to take my mind off things. After a cup of tea, a pint of orange juice and a four-egg omelette I got showered and changed, ready for my first day at my new job.

Michael turned up with the car and tooted the horn outside my gaff about nine. I grabbed my suit jacket and skipped down the stairs, thoughts of the exotic Heidi still swimming about in my brain.

'Good weekend mate?' asked Michael.

'Yeh, cracking, met a gorgeous black bird.'

'Aye? Gone native have we, heh heh. Better watch out she don't put a voodoo curse on you Taff.'

'Shut up butt. I tell you mun, she is sexy as fuck. Wait 'till you see her.'

'Can't wait boyo. Can't wait.'

*

Everyone knew the boss had a smart bird and a sweet, little baby daughter but few people ever saw them. Apparently she was a bit of a looker and Patrick didn't want any of his testosterone-fuelled lads getting ideas above their station. Not that anyone ever would of course. We all knew that would be the quickest way to a death sentence, preceded by a nasty bit of genital torture but that didn't stop the boss being as paranoid as a nigger on a rape charge.

Michael had first met the missus when she returned to the city a couple of years back and was surprised at how fast she'd moved in.

'Go on then. Tell me, what's she like? No bullshit either,' I asked.

'Well, didn't take her long.'

'For what?'

'Shacked up with him just about straight away. She's originally from this area you see. Knew the family. Her ma did a runner years ago but when she croaked her ladyship came back home. Whirlwind romance as they say in the movies, they got hitched, nice Caribbean island for the honeymoon, Antigua I believe it was. Wasn't long after she got back to London.'

'Came back from where?'

'Ha ha, funny enough your part of the world believe it or not.'

The hairs on the back of my neck were standing up

now. It couldn't be, could it?

We pulled up in the motor, the tyres crunching over the gravel on the driveway, and got out.

'You alright Paul?' asks Michael. 'You look a bit clammy mate.'

'Yeh, grand,' I lie.

'Think your African queen must have sapped your strength Samson,' he said.

Michael puts a stubby finger on the doorbell and I'm listening to some tubular bells-type ringtone shit that grates on me from the first note. It feels like an age before it's answered but eventually the large oak door slowly swings open and there she is.

I nearly throw up on the spot but manage to cough into my hand, wishing a big hole will open up and swallow me.

Charley ignores me, like I was invisible, and invites the pair of us inside.

'Coffee boys?' she offers.

'Only if you're having one miss,' replies Michael as subserviently as he can without bowing. 'If it's not too much trouble,' he adds quickly.

'Yeh, nay bother. Take your jackets off, grab a seat,' she says and points to the front room and a large, four-seater white leather sofa.

I didn't know what to do. I felt like I was in a film that had already finished. Like everyone knew the ending except me. I stared at my shoes in a daze until she returned with two mugs of Kenya's best.

'Right lads, drop the bullshit, I won't bite. He's away so just call me Charley alright.'

'Yes miss,' we both stumbled.

'Great. When you've finished those I'll get my coat, you can drop me in town.'

The drive into Covent Garden was the longest of my life. I sat staring out the side window while Michael negotiated the heavy traffic. Every now and then I glanced across and saw Michael eyeing me up in between checking our precious cargo in the rear view mirror. I felt so guilty I thought the whole world knew but it was only my nerves.

'So what's your name boyo?'

'Paul miss.'

'Nice name,' she leaned forward, turned her head towards me and winked her left eye.

'Thanks,' I spluttered.

'Been with the firm long then?'

'No miss. About a year or so I guess.'

'I lived in Wales once,' said Charley.

'Yeh, what part?' I was begging for her to shut up. I just wanted to go home, ring Heidi, drown my sorrows and bury my head in her chocolate cleavage to take my mind off the horrendous ache in my stomach.

'Cardiff. Little city, full of little boys.'

A bit uncalled for I thought but I grunted my agreement.

Michael pulled up sharply as a group of anti-apartheid demonstrators blocked the road outside the South African Embassy.

'Feckin' eejits,' he shouted out the window.

'Take me to Neals Yard first yeh. Rough Trade record shop.'

'Yes miss.'

'Then Harrods.'

'Okay.'

'I'm meeting the girls in Rowley Leigh's Kensington Place for lunch so you can have the afternoon off I guess.'

'We'll wait miss.'

'Okay, suit yourself but I'm not bringing you a doggy bag,' she joked.

'We'll be fine miss,' said Michael.

*

We dropped off Charley and then found a spot to park up. It was cold outside and the huge sky seemed torn by the wind as grey clouds edged menacingly across the heavens above us. Every now and again sunlight leaked through and flared into our eyes as it reflected off the harsh glass and metal of the city.

'Seems she took a shine to you mate,' said Michael, breaking the silence in the motor.

'Nah I doubt it,' I lied. 'Perhaps she heard my accent. Reminded her of Wales I imagine.'

'Aye, maybe,' agreed Michael, although I wasn't sure he believed me. He was a clever bastard that one.

Fourteen

The following day we had the morning off but Charley had decided she wanted to go clubbing in the night with one of her old school friends so it was our job to take them out, make sure no-one got within twenty feet of them and then bring the pair back home safely.

'Let's take her to one of our clubs yeh? It'll be safer,' suggests Michael.

'Definitely,' I agree.

'Hi boys. This is Cara, an old friend,' said Charley as she waltzed through the living room door with her stunning friend in tow.

'Hello,' we smiled in unison. "We were thinking of taking you to...'

'The Astoria, in Soho,' Cara interrupted.

'Oh no sorry miss... that's a bit too dangerous...'

'Great idea love, let's go get 'em.'

'Oh fuck,' mumbled Michael under his breath.

*

First opened in 1976 the Astoria was one of the biggest clubs in eighties London and hosted some of the best bands of the time with Oasis and the Manic Street Preachers playing there.

It was just before Christmas and we knew it would be a logistical nightmare having to play bodyguard to these beauties but we had no other choice. We toyed with the idea of phoning a few of the other lads to tag along but when Charley produced four tickets to Nirvana we knew we'd been stitched up good and proper.

The concert was mental although a bit loud for my tastes and Kurt was on great form. Luckily for us the crowd was mostly long-haired youngsters far more interested in the band than any of us golden oldies and after the gig we did manage to persuade them to head back north and to a more discreet venue.

All was quiet on the western front until I leave the girls with Michael to take a leak. I get to the toilets and there's this dick blocking the doorway. There's a line of customers queuing up as well, all too scared to do anything.

'Oi buttie, out of the way,' I shout above the heads of the people waiting in line.

'Who says?' comes the reply.

'Excuse me miss. Excuse me sir. Can I just squeeze through there love…'

When I've made my way through the crowd, 'People want to get passed mate.'

'So what?' says mister prize penis head as he tenses his arm across the corridor now.

I'm incredibly patient for about half a second. Then I slowly lean in.

'Move your fuckin' arm before I break the fuckin' thing in six places you cunt.'

'What?'

I grab his arm and twist it backwards rapidly. His knees buckle as he tries to stop his forearm breaking and he *accidentally* head-butts my left hook, which knocks him to the floor.

Releasing his arm I encourage the waiting crowd to

pass us by. He is not happy with the audience seeing him on his arse so jumps up off the carpet to square up to me. He pushes his chest out and is about to say something clever when I lean in even closer than last time so he can smell my breath and truly feel the warmth of my kind words.

'If I were you sonny I'd fuck off while you still have legs that work.'

He realises his mistake and shuffles off, tail between his legs, muttering something under his breath. I have no idea why he was blocking the path to the bogs. I guess some people just do that?

I take a leak in a cubicle with the door locked, in case he decides to jump me from behind and then walk out. Outside the door are four adorable Spanish birds jabbering away nineteen to the dozen and pointing at me.

The first one smiles at me and slides an arm around my waist. 'Thank you big mister,' she says seductively, gesturing towards the ladies sign.

'He was stalking our friend,' the other girl chips in. 'How can we repay you? You're our heroico,' she adds in her deep and sensual European voice.

It's tempting but I politely decline the offer of five-ups or whatever it's called and after a brief chat and four big wet kisses on my cheek I make my way back to Charley and company.

Returning to the table I notice Michael has his tongue down the throat of Cara while Charley winks at me.

'Been touching up your make up Paul?'
'Wha'?'

Charley points at my face and smirks.

'Oh shit, yeh. No, I mean...' I stutter.

Now at that precise moment I didn't know what to do. Give me a few thugs to fight rather than have me try to work out what is going on in a woman's mind any day.

Charley sensed my anxiety though and ushered me to the other side of her seat.

'Look Paul. Sorry about everything. I'll explain when we can get a few minutes alone together.'

'It's alright,' I attempt to answer without sounding choked up but I fail.

*

It's getting late and Charley decides it's time Cara was safely tucked up in bed. Michael wasn't arguing and was keen to do the tucking, with a capital F.

'Right lads, let's go,' she commanded.

We stepped outside and being the only sober one there I was soon called upon to help out again.

A drunken woman was stood in front of us as we exited the club. As she tried to flag a taxi down she began to topple over, in slow motion, into the path of the oncoming cars.

I rushed out and pulled her back onto the pavement just before she hit the deck and got creamed by a passing black cab. People die regularly like that on London roads. I propped her down, made her sit against a wall until I'd flagged another taxi down to pour her into.

'Such a gentleman,' slurred Michael, smiling.

'Aye, bob a job me init,' I replied.

I couldn't help notice Charley stealing a glance at me and smirking as we walked to our nearby car. I wouldn't mind but I wasn't even supposed to be working the door anymore and it was supposed to be an easy job this.

Ah well so much for career progression in this game.

Fifteen

The festive season passed without too much hassle. Patrick had returned from his business trips and was back running his growing empire from a bar off the A1 road. He seemed to have little time for Charley and their baby daughter, a pretty little thing called Morgan.

The days were reasonably relaxing. Michael and I would often just be hanging around, driving here and there, taking Charley to the hairdressers, to a local fitness club for her weekly aerobics class and occasionally to a pub for dinner.

On days when Charley didn't want to go anywhere we either had the day off or we just lounged about the mansion drinking espresso coffee from this fancy machine they had.

There was a big garden behind the kitchen and a high brick wall with barbed wire on the top. I used to inspect the boundaries, wave at the cameras, check for blind spots near the row of mature trees at the back. I'd never seen a house like it. How the other half live.

There was also a huge lawn that was covered with plastic, jungle gym type equipment for the little girl to play on. If I got the chance I would happily spend the day pushing her on a swing, which sure as hell beat door work, minding or enforcement.

*

Looking back I guess I was still a tad naïve as far as what the firm were up to. I knew they ran several pubs and the clubs of course. I knew they controlled the drugs that flowed through this part of the city and was fairly comfortable with a bit of protection or gambling but what I was oblivious too were the other activities that went hand in hand with this way of life, namely; loan sharking, armed robbery, prostitution, arms dealing and even human trafficking.

If I'd known then what I came to know later, would I have left? Probably. But at the time I didn't really see it. I still had rose-coloured glasses on, assumed the people that got hurt deserved it for trying to muscle in on the boss's turf. The truth, as with all organised crime was far less palatable.

———— *

As the year passed Michael and myself were still enjoying the high times in the swinging city with only the odd bit of aggravation to sort when someone stepped out of line, which wasn't very often such was Patrick's growing reputation as a boss you did not fuck about with.

I remember a few times we took Charley and her friends to a venue on Wardour Street called The Wag Club. This was a time when London's music and club scene was the melting pot for artists, bands and fashion designers that would later become icons of British culture. Welshman Steve Strange, famous gender-bender Boy George, Jean-Paul Gaultier, Neneh Cherry, George Michael, Keith Richards, Joe Strummer, Robert De Niro, Prince and Madonna would all hang out there. David Bowie even filmed the video for 'Blue Jean' at the club.

Charley loved to party alright and with a different musical genre blaring out every night of the week I was soon becoming an expert on jazz, funk, reggae, hip-hop, house and acid.

Michael was also enjoying himself as he slowly made his way through most of Charley's friends while I did eventually get to chat to her about what was going on in her life and more importantly, why she'd left me back in Cardiff a few years earlier.

We had to be careful as Michael hardly ever left me alone with her for long but slowly but surely we snatched a few conversations together.

*

'Look Paul, I'm sorry, it was really complicated alright.'

'Yeh, whatever you say,' I snapped back but instantly regretted it as I saw Charley was upset.

The kettle clicked off and she poured water into three mugs with teabags.

'He found out where I was. We went out a bit before I met you, I told you. When I used to pop back to London to see the girls.'

'So where did I come in?' I asked.

'Oh don't. Not now. Patrick is jealous as hell, you can't say or do anything.' Charley stirred the tea and her big tawny-brown eyes begged me to understand.

'I gathered that,' I giggled nervously.

'I don't love him Paul...' she replied, as my gaze freewheeled down to the bronzed, perfectly toned legs.

'Really?'

'No. You know I don't but he threatened me. It's you I...'

'What? How do you mean?' I interrupted.

'Forget it Paul. You don't understand what he's like. He's a total psycho, but he treats me well now. I got this huge pad, my beautiful Morgan. She likes you I see,' she smiled, trying to change the subject but I couldn't help feel the rage rising within me.

'So what am I supposed to do?' I begged.

'Just be here for me. In case I need you yeh...'

'I can't. It's too difficult. I'll have to quit and...'

'No, I...'

'Oi, boyo, come on, hurry up, Frank wants us uptown,' Michael burst into the kitchen where me and Charley were standing far too close to each other.

*

As the weeks went by I noticed that Michael and I were getting called away from the house a lot. We learned a few of the other lads had taken a pasting from a rival gang from further east and Patrick wanted to be sure he had enough muscle on tap to nip any possible trouble in the bud.

His drug empire was growing fast and tales of extreme violence were filtering down to all of us, making a few of the older lads a bit jumpy.

Violence has levels. One on one, most blokes will fight until one of them draws blood, loses a tooth, gets their nose broke or something. Most pub or street fights are like this. That's all well and good until you come up against a guy that won't stop until you're unconscious or worse. Then come weapons; bats, bars and all manner of implements that tend to be harder than flesh and bone.

Next up is blades. As soon as you get steel it's a whole new ball game. It's incredibly easy to kill someone with a few inches of metal. If it goes into your heart you're dead, simple as. And then come guns of course.

The main problem I saw with the drug trade was that there was so much money to be made that the criminal arms race went out of control. Gangs upped the ante not only to make the cash in the first place but also to protect it from being taken from them later on.

The grass was coming in from Morocco mostly. It was easy enough for most crews to get into. But in the early nineties it all changed when cocaine started to become more popular. When the South Americans started supplying the UK the stakes were upped big time. At first they would only deal with well-connected, known faces, like Patrick, but as time went on everyone got involved. It was getting a bit out of hand for me and I'd wished I'd stayed green in Cardiff.

The smuggling routes were well sorted by this time and the distribution networks were also set up satisfactorily. I heard we got our product through the embassies and diplomatic bags. The cops couldn't touch it so it was all fairly hassle free.

Another difference in the cocaine back then was the quality. It was virtually one hundred per cent pure. The suppliers wanted to get people hooked so they gave us really good shit. It was only as the years went on that it got cut with stuff like washing powder and laxatives.

Of course me and Michael never touched it. I was known to hate drugs so the other boys were happy to keep me away from that side of things anyway and Michael was a simple Budweiser and birds sort of bloke. Having said that he was still remarkably knowledgeable when it came to the history of the trade and I always enjoyed our little sojourns into drug culture and his yarns about all the famous people who partook of a line or three.

'Shackleton was one mate,' proclaimed Michael.

'What? The polar explorer? No way mun!'

'Aye, they used to take this stuff called *Forced March*; full of feckin' coke that was. No wonder he managed to row across the feckin' southern ocean eh! I bet they fed it to the penguins too, watch the little bastards swim around in circles!'

'Piss off you nutter.'

'It's true boyo, I shit you not.'

'And what about Coca Cola?' I asked.

'Yeh, far as I know. There was about sixty milligrams of the white stuff in that particular pick me up tonic, heh heh.'

I laughed along, amazed this big, not so thick Irishman knew so much. Life was good. I was getting a free education and tons of cash. I'd started saving too; four or five instant access building society accounts where I had a few grand stashed away in each one.

After me and Charley's stolen chats I still wasn't comfortable living and working for a violent hoodlum. Deep down I knew I had to escape and try to eek out a safer, quieter life for myself somewhere. It was easier said than done though. You didn't just walk away from this sort of crap.

*

Michael and I were sat on a large table for four at the back of the pub. It was lunchtime and there were a lot of people waiting to find somewhere to sit in order to get something to eat. People glanced in our direction, then thought twice about joining us. Nobody seemed to want to sit anywhere near us in fact. Punters would walk in, wander up to where we were sat, take one look and then walk away. Office workers would be talking loudly as they moved between tables and then abruptly went quiet before turning around. I was getting used to empty chairs for company.

'Listen Taff, we have to watch our backs alright?' advised Michael one night.

'Of course mate.'

'No, you're not listening. I mean it. Patrick is losing it I reckon. He's getting himself in a right state. The kind of life he lives, he's bound to be a bit wound up yeh? And he's using again.'

'The boss? Never!'

'Aye and spending too much time off your face is just going to make the paranoia worse. He must have put the value of a good sized semi-detached up his nose this last twelve months.'

'Shit.'

'I've seen it before. It gets in your blood. The

violence just builds up, surrounded by it every day. Trying to keep one step ahead of the Old Bill is one thing but this game is not healthy. It's getting lawless out there.'

'So what shall we do?' I asked.

'And there's more.'

'What?'

'I overheard him talking to Frank last week. He's jealous of all the time we're spending round the missus.'

'What? But he sends us there?'

'Yeh I know. Someone told him you're an honest guy in a scrape. That you'd take a kicking to save her. He trusts you that way. Trouble is he doesn't trust you the other way, know what I mean boyo.'

'I wouldn't,' I lied.

'And your good around the kid too. Big softie aren't you eh?'

'Fuck off.'

Michael had a point though. I loved the little bundle alright. Morgan was cute as fuck.

'Well it's nice to get away from the serious shit for a while innit,' I defended myself.

'Yeh, she's a cracking little kid to be sure.'

Michael was giving me his all-knowing look again. I had no idea why.

'Look Taff, I like you, but this racket is changing. If I were you I'd get out while you can. Tell the boss your granddad's dog is dying or something. Say you need a break. Hide out down the mines for a bit, heh heh.'

'Alright, I'll think about it. Thanks mate.'

Sixteen

1991

As the new decade dawned so the drug trade continued to grow. So did the number of dealers. Everyone was at it. You might have thought the extra competition was a bad thing but in reality it was an opportunity for Patrick.

We started off by taxing the smaller dealers, as it was called back then. What this entailed was finding out where the flats or houses were that held the cash or drugs and then simply robbing them. Often we just posed as buyers, knocked the front door and when it opened up you kicked the chain off the wall and thrust saw-offs into their faces. Sometimes you pretended there was an accident and you needed to use a phone, same thing really. Blitzkrieg the flat, in fast and hard. Don't give them a chance to think about standing up to you and take everything at gunpoint, including any jewellery or fancy watches they had on.

If you rushed in quick, knocked them to the floor, tied them up while shooters were pointed at their heads there wasn't much they could do, or even wanted to do, about it. Sometimes they'd mouth off but a quick smack to the face or the back of the head and it usually did the trick and they quickly quietened down. Occasionally pickings were slim, other times you got thousands. If you had the time you'd watch a place until you knew plenty of money had gone in. After the weekend was a good time. Also, many of the smaller crooks regularly used their own product so on Monday morning they weren't at their best.

Stoned and knackered they rarely put up much opposition.

The easy pickings didn't last long though for as news went around that dealers were being robbed so they started arming themselves and it became more dangerous. Another form of crime exhausted so we then started offering protection to the same people we'd robbed in previous months. We told them we'd supply them and stop anyone else taxing them! You had to stay one step ahead of the trends I guess.

*

It was about this time I started to really see what drugs did to someone and it turned my stomach. I decided I was going to work for another year or two and then get out. If that was even possible.

Me, Michael and two other lads had been given an address to rob. We watched from outside for a few hours, just in case it was a setup, then saw a few young lads going in. Ten minutes later they were back out, smiling and laughing.

'Okay, looks good,' said Michael. 'Shall we go?'

'Aye, why not.'

It was my turn to knock the door. We often tossed a coin as the first guy in was always in most danger, especially if the occupants were drugged up, armed and jumpy. Shoot first ask questions later some silly folks.

I rapped my knuckles hard on the door and waited.

The door soon opened and it was like looking at a ghost. I hesitated. Michael didn't, he pushed the door ajar and rushed in with the other lads, Sean and Cian.

The girl was knocked to the floor and as the others rushed around the flat I helped the young girl to her feet. She must have been about fifteen but looked forty. Big pink and grey bruises under her sunken eyes, scrawny arms with scabs and track marks everywhere.

We didn't find anything and just left her sitting there on the only piece of furniture in the flat, a stinking, flower-patterned sofa in the middle of the room. The threadbare carpet had bloody syringes, used condoms, cigarette packets, drinks cans and even human shit all over it. The place stank.

'Come on, leave the skank alone,' shouted Michael as they walked away.

'Hang on, I'll catch you up.'

I'd seen plenty of crappy bedsits and junkies but this was the first time I'd seen the true effects of heroin addiction so up close and personal. I didn't like it one bit.

'Are you alright love?' I asked.

She seemed to be in a daze. Her limp eyes seemed to follow me around the room but unexpectedly she snapped out of it and went for my trousers, hands trying to undo my belt.

'Whoa, take it easy,' I shouted.

She slumped down and seemed disappointed.

'Give me a fiver and I'll give you a blowjob,' she begged.

'Fuckin' hell. No thanks love. Do you want a cup of tea?'

She started laughing. The giggles quickly turned to tears, then violence. She lunged at me with her nails. I instinctively swatted her to the floor and watched as her battered and bruised body scattered a few empty beer cans about the place.

She simply lay there motionless, like a human puddle of bones. Her clothes were filthy and I wanted to call an ambulance but before I could pick her up and check she was okay I felt Sean's strong grip. He grabbed my arm and pulled me to the door.

'Come on Taff, we're needed elsewhere. The boss can't get hold of Frank. He's worried it might be serious too.'

Seventeen

On the drive to the meet with Frank and two of the other lads Michael gave us all another history lesson.

'Okay, so although crack cocaine had been invented in Holland around the late seventies it wasn't until about nineteen eighty-three when the drug started making an appearance in Miami. It then quickly moved up the east coast to New York and the west side to Los Angeles.'

'So who started making it?' asked Cian, from the back seat.

Michael continued, 'I'll get to that in a minute.'

'Sorry.'

'Where was I? Oh yeh right... so it decimated the inner city areas, especially the black ghettos and poorer parts of the US cities. In less than five years, so by about nineteen eighty-eight, the murder rate was up, teenage dealers were shooting at the police and almost all violent crime was drug-related.'

'And that's what's coming here? Happy days boys,' I added.

'So are the Yardies making it or are they just selling this crap?' asked Cian again.

'Aye, well no, it's the Columbians who produce it. The spades just deal. The South Americans used to sell cocaine to the rich, white middle-classes and were always on the lookout for a new product and market. They knew from experience that to increase volume all they had to do was get the underprivileged black community hooked and they'd be quids in. The problem was that cocaine was

99

expensive so they needed a cheaper, more addictive drug. With crack they found the golden ticket.'

'So it's coke for the hard-up then?' said Cian.

'Charlie for the chocolate factory,' I added.

'Yeh, pretty much,' replied Michael and everyone laughed.

'How is it different to powder then? How is it made?'

'It's easy to make. Crack is produced when you dissolve cocaine in ammonia, add water and bicarb, then boil off the liquid. You're left with rocks of crack. Problem is it's feckin' dangerous to do. Often explodes in your face I hear.'

'Sounds delightful.'

'Yeh but for addicts it's the business. The high from smoking it is huge and instant. It works by interfering with the dopamine systems in the brain and lasts several minutes, unlike pure powder, which can last a few hours. The problem with crack is that it is extremely addictive, almost instantly so, and users want a new fix more or less straight away. Addicts have reported that in just a few days of use they were completely hooked. It's the perfect drug for dealers to make maximum profit.'

'What's a dope-a-fuckin'-mean?' asked Cian.

'You mate,' said Michael.

'Yippee-feckin'-do,' said Sean, who was the strong silent type.

*

By the late eighties most of the UK's big cities had various black gangs starting to push crack. North London was no exception and as long as they stuck to their own patch Patrick was happy, but as time went on they started to expand and encroach on his manor. This he didn't like and wasn't prepared to tolerate.

In early 1991 he'd agreed to a meet to sort out some kind of access for a cut of the profits but the meeting didn't go well. The up and coming black gangs were a different breed. Many of them were from Jamaica, arriving in the UK on false passports, with extreme violence never far behind.

We started to see a whole new level of grotesque and didn't like it one bit. I was fine with my fists but seeing swords, handguns and automatic weapons was scary stuff. Was Michael right? Did I really need this shit? Maybe the time had come for me to disappear.

*

As it turned out the tip-off about the drugs in the flat was a decoy. To try to entice a few of us away from a deal Frank was setting up in an old disused warehouse off the main road in Cambridge Heath, not far from Bethnal Green. They wanted us a few men down as, unbeknown to us at the time, a rival south London gang was going to try to take Patrick out.

Unfortunately for them, Patrick didn't show. He was out with Charley for once and so wasn't on the scene. He'd sent Frank along as he didn't consider it was anything much to worry about. Patrick's growing hubris and his perceived self importance was starting to go to his head and when me and the other three boys turned up it was already all over.

Michael stopped the car across the road, more or less out of line of sight. We observed the aftermath of the slaughter from a distance for a few minutes. Then we saw bodies being carried into the back of a transit van. Michael's old mobile, a Motorola MicroTAC, wasn't working properly so Sean leapt out of the car and ran to a nearby phone box to tell Patrick the bad news.

Patrick would never normally have involved Charley in his business but for some reason she was still with him this time. He'd been collecting a bit of protection money and the takings from a few clubs. It was only going to take him an hour so Charley tagged along as they wanted to go to a new restaurant she'd heard about and it saved doubling back in the nightmare London traffic.

So as Patrick was driving himself and Charley home his Nokia Cityman rang. He liked to keep up with the times and felt super important now he was contactable most of the time thanks to these crazy new inventions that would eventually change the world of business, finance and organised crime forever.

No doubt off his face on coke Patrick committed the cardinal error – don't mix business with pleasure and always keep your private life separate from the day job. Instead of simply dropping Charley off so she could grab a cab home he spun the car around and headed to the crime scene, where we were still watching and waiting.

'How many Michael?' I asked.

'Got to be at least four or five I reckon.'

'Shit. Armed yeh?'

'No, they just topped Frank with harsh language. Course they're feckin' tooled up you prick!' shouted Michael, anger getting the better of him for once.

None of us had any idea what the meeting was about, although Cian did mention that Patrick was supposed to have been there but pulled out at the last minute. He said Charley had asked to see him about something important although he didn't know what.

The spades that had ambushed Frank and his two bodyguards were arguing amongst themselves when Patrick turned up. Red as a beetroot and wound up to fuck he jumped from his Merc and ran to the back where he opened the boot and pulled out a shotgun.

'Whoa, Patrick,' said Sean, as he stood in his way, attempting to calm the boss down.

'Get out of my feckin' way. Tell the lads. We're going to get some payback.'

'Shouldn't we get more bodies boss,' asked Michael, 'There's at least five of the black fuckers in there.'

'Five of them, five of us. I'll take those odds any day,' said Patrick. 'Come on,' he spat and strode off towards the old building.

In this game you had to keep your eye on the ball twenty-four seven. Soon as you relaxed the shit would hit the fan. Patrick was using heavy and was unpredictable now. It was a recipe for disaster and the lads knew it too.

Michael threw me a crowbar as the other lads had grabbed all the guns and I glanced quickly at Charley in the passenger seat of Patrick's Mercedes as she mouthed. 'Be careful.'

The thing I've learned about taking someone out,

whether it's with a punch or a bullet is you need a couple of things. First and foremost – surprise. If you get the first hit in you'll probably win. The second thing was total, one hundred per cent belief that you were walking away and not the other guy. With that in mind I guess there was another point to consider and that was aggression. Pure, unadulterated aggression. You moved fast and hard and didn't stop going for it until it was all over.

We crossed the open waste ground quickly and were now alongside the warehouse wall. We very nearly had surprise on our side until Cian accidentally kicked an old pop bottle. It skidded across the concrete yard we were quietly skulking across, leaving us suddenly feeling very exposed. The black gang ahead of us were jumpy as fuck. They'd just murdered three guys, in cold blood, the adrenaline would be pumping through them, they were bound to be coked up and would think they were superhuman, not to mention bulletproof.

The first shot hit Sean in the eye. He dropped instantly as Michael returned the favour and popped one into the stomach of Sean's killer. Patrick blasted away and winged two guys as all hell broke loose.

Cian sprinted after one bloke who'd decided to make a run for it. He caught up with him quickly and shot him, fatally, in the back. The darkie hit the deck but rolled over and incredibly got straight back up. He turned to face Cian as another bullet ripped through his arm. He managed to return fire as he fell for the second and final time. Cian got hit in the leg, just below the knee and screamed as he crumpled onto the ground.

By a weird stroke of luck the only other black guy

left standing was like me, unarmed, apart from a poxy knife. I'd already sized him up as the rest of the gun-fight was being played out all around us.

I ran straight for him as he held the blade out in front, waving it from side to side until my crowbar knocked it from his hand. I'd learnt in Cardiff, which had its fair share of black guys, that you never punched one in the head, you went for the solar plexus instead. Instinct must have kicked in because I head-butted the bastard in the belly. He groaned as we both went down but I was quicker getting back into the fight. I sprang back to my feet and swung the iron bar. As he tried to rise I connected with his chin with the force of a truck. I heard a loud crack and he fell backwards unconscious, possibly even dead.

Meanwhile, Patrick had quickly reloaded and killed one of the injured blokes he'd clipped first with a blast to the head. His skull shattered and blood and brains covered the rough concrete floor. He was now pointing his weapon at the other guy, who was sat down, holding a bloody shoulder wound. Patrick was grinning like an idiot. I'd seen that look before and it chilled me.

'Paul! Look out!' screamed Charley barely a few yards off to the side of me as the guy Michael had shot had managed to get to his feet and was now trying to point a handgun at me with a shaking hand.

Michael had run after Cian and was helping him limp back to us when Patrick swiftly turned away from the guy he was guarding and fired.

'Fuck no!' I screamed.

The next few moments played out like a slow

motion film. One that couldn't be paused or halted. I had entered a strange dream-like state. Feeling utterly detached from reality and unable to intervene.

'Oh Paul...'

Patrick had swung around too quickly and not looked where he was aiming. The stupid prick had just pulled the trigger as Charley ran into the line of fire to try to warn me. She was hit full force.

The injured guy on the floor seized his opportunity, got up and punched Patrick in the back of the neck from behind and ran off. The bloke who was pointing a gun at me also followed suit and scarpered, holding his wounded stomach. As Patrick fell to his knees he looked up to see me running to where Charley lay. I gathered her up in my arms.

She had been hit in the chest and there was blood everywhere.

'Help me, Paul,' she mumbled.

'It's alright love, I'll get you to hospital, hang on, you'll be fine,' I replied.

It was then I noticed the holes in Charley's blouse. There were half a dozen or more, closely packed. She'd taken a shotgun blast to her centre mass from less than ten yards away.

'Charley? Wake up!' I started to shake her fragile, blood-soaked body.

I watched the light go out of her beautiful brown eyes as they slowly closed and she fell limp in my arms.

'No, Charley, no!' I cried out loud but knew it was over. Nobody survived a point blank hit like that.

'You cunt,' screamed Patrick as he staggered

towards me and stared down at his dead wife. 'I'll feckin' kill you.'

I carefully laid Charley's tattered body down on the hard ground and slowly rose to my feet. Patrick's eyes went black as he raised his weapon but I knew he was out of cartridges. I punched him as hard as I'd ever hit anyone. I saw his eyes shut and he slumped to the ground. I kicked him a few good ones in the bollocks and then straightened up.

Michael was staring at me, while I could see Cian was moaning, head down, sat on the floor and propped against the wall.

'Fuck,' was all Michael said.

In his hand he held a sawn-off, casually down by his side.

'Make a decision mate. Make it quick though,' I said through gritted teeth, resigned to accept my fate at that precise moment and not giving two fucks whether I lived or died.

He regarded me for a second, saw Cian was out of it with the pain and in all probability hadn't seen or heard anything. Michael could see Patrick was out cold so he was the only witness.

'Sorry,' he said softly and pointed towards the Merc with his free arm. He knew in that brief moment, by the shell-shocked look on my face and the fact Charley had called my name not Patrick's, all he ever needed to know.

'See ya then. Take care buttie,' I replied and walked to the car.

'You too, good luck,' said Michael. He paused for

a second then added, 'You know we'll be coming.'
    'Aye mate. I know.'

Eighteen

After less than fifteen minutes driving west I pulled the Merc into a quiet side street. I checked the back seat and grabbed a jacket of Patrick's. It was a bit small but it would do. Outside I lifted the boot of the luxury car to discover a bulging, brown Adidas holdall and a few tools. I unzipped the sports bag about half way to reveal wads of cash. I didn't bother counting it but knew there was a lot of money in there. I quickly added a few tools, zipped the bag back up and closed the boot.

I took the keys with me, walked a few yards before throwing them into a hedge as I crossed the road. I checked directions, twice each way, did my green cross code then strode out confidently. My steps were measured, like a child might do when faced with a huge expanse of open road. I didn't run, instead I moved like an army explosives expert, a member of the UXB unit, walking calmly away from a lit fuse.

My mind was racing, my heart was pumping fast and I was crying like a baby deep down inside but through all these emotions I knew one thing. I had to keep moving.

Then it occurred to me that I was dead. A dead man walking anyway. It was purely a matter of time. Patrick was far too arrogant to blame himself or even believe it was an accident. He was way too conceited for that, plus he had appearances to keep up and Michael had heard Charley call out my name, loud and clear. He would want revenge big time and there was only one person he was going to blame for this tragedy and it wasn't fuckin' Dave Allen. It was me.

Even though I knew it was bad it hadn't truly registered with me. The woman I loved, the only woman I'd ever really loved was gone. My beautiful warm Charley was lying in a pool of blood, cold as a stone.

Luckily for me though my survival mechanism had kicked in automatically. I wanted to be with her. I wanted to hold her, do something, anything, but it was too late. I had to get away from there quickly. Far from there, far from that ugly place.

First I had to get out of the city. There were the usual ways; car, bus or train. Most routes would be covered by Patrick's men in half an hour so I had to move fast but I also had to think. There were four directions; north south, east or west. Everyone would bank on me heading west, back to Wales, like a dog with its tail between its legs. A fleeing rat, bolting for the safety of the nest. Back home. That's where everyone ran. I decided that would have to be my first big no-no.

East was out too, I didn't fancy going to France either, they would have men at the ports who would be looking out for me anyway. South was an option, down to Brighton maybe, but it wasn't far enough away as far as I was concerned.

Although I still felt as muddled as fuck I somehow managed to keep it together long enough to jog to the nearest outdoor car park I could find. Walking casually up and down the rows of cars I finally spotted a vehicle that might be easy to nick. I selected an old Ford Fiesta that didn't look like it was alarmed and was tucked away in a corner of the lot. I used the crowbar I now had stuffed inside my jacket to smash the driver's window in. I stuck my hand in, flicked the catch to unlock the car, opened the door and got in. The car had manual winders so I quickly wound down the window so you couldn't see the glass if anyone happened to be passing.

A few miles away I can hear the first sirens. I watched as two cop cars went hurtling past me, blue lights flashing. They might have been going anywhere but odds were they had been called when shots were heard by someone near the warehouse. With any luck they would slow Patrick and his goons down a bit as they would have to distance themselves from the earlier mayhem too.

Quickly levering the plastic cover from underneath the dash I exposed the steering column and saw the wires I was looking for. I'd never hot wired a car before but had seen it done a couple of times so pulled as many of the wires out as I could.

There were a few bundles and I knew I needed the ones going into the steering column. I unclipped them and was faced with five different coloured wires. I needed three; ignition, battery and starter. Using the Swiss Army pocket knife I always carried I set to work fraying the insulation until I exposed the bare metal enclosed within. I connected the ignition and battery wires, winding them around each other and touched the bare starter wire to them.

The car fired straight away and I pressed the accelerator a bit to rev the engine. I noticed I had slightly over half a tank of petrol on the dashboard display, which would be plenty.

Lastly, I moved the starter wire away from the other two and bent it back on itself so it wouldn't hit the live wires again as I drove. I cracked the steering lock like I would have snapped Patrick's head if I could have got near the bastard and I was soon in gear and pulling slowly away.

Leaving the car park I drove as slow as I could at first, desperate to try to calm my nerves. The adrenaline was still coursing through my veins as I scanned all around, checked left and right, then my rear view mirror and tried hard to control my breathing as I edged gently into traffic and headed for Hendon Way and Brent Cross.

When I reached the M1 I pushed on up to sixty-five miles an hour and cruised along with my arm out the window. I dug out a few cassette tapes from the glove compartment and stuck a Gerry Rafferty album in the car stereo. *Take The Money and Run* blasted out the speakers. So far so good...

An hour or two later, when I reached signs for Nottingham, I pulled off the motorway and into the services. I'd succeeded in putting a fair bit of distance between myself and London but what the hell was I going to do next? I needed more time to deliberate. I parked up out of sight of the café and pulled the wires apart and stopped the engine.

I picked up as much of the glass as I could and chucked it out of the window. Taking the holdall from the passenger seat I stuck it in the boot, seeing as the window was now permanently open. After leaving the car I turned my own blood-soaked jacket inside out and hung it across the steering wheel to hide the mess underneath and prayed the car hadn't been reported stolen yet.

Luckily, I had about a grand in my jeans, in fifty-pound notes, plus twenty or thirty thousand in the sports bag so I figured I was alright for a year or two at least. As long as I kept my head down and could find somewhere quiet to hide out maybe I'd be safe.

I quickly dashed into the toilets and checked my face and clothes. I wiped a speck of blood from my cheek. Whose was it? The food and coffee I'd ordered didn't much resemble the colourful fare in the ad papered on the services restaurant window but it would have to do. I found a quiet place to sit in a corner booth. I can't say I enjoyed it going down but knew I must get calories and energy inside me.

Returning to the toilet cubicle I was violently sick. I practically crawled back to the car, feeling as weak as a wet leaf. All I could think of was poor Charley, lying there. Not moving. I kept telling myself she was okay, that maybe it appeared worse than it was, that they would have got her to hospital... but soon the realisation came flooding back. She was dead, there was no going back and I was now in some very serious, deep shit.

Nineteen

Back in north London the gang had regrouped and everyone was waiting for orders from Patrick, who was nursing a huge shiner and a broken nose. He was also limping around due to his swollen balls.

'Look, I want that big fucker tracked down and brought to me.'

'Aye boss but what about the spades?' asked Michael.

'Yeh, yeh, we'll deal with them too. I want Frank and the lads avenged as much as you all do, but priority must be that feckin' Taff. I knew I couldn't trust him.'

Michael and the other lads gathered around, bowed their heads and nodded, although rumour was it wasn't really his fault. Michael had discreetly suggested Charley's death might have been an accident. Patrick, on the other hand, was desperately trying to convince everyone it was down to one man – the Welsh man.

'Boss, we have to protect the firm first. We can always find Paul later, where can he go? He'll hide out somewhere, probably amongst the sheep and cows. We'll get him, but first we need to sort things closer to home, yeh?'

'My dead feckin' wife close enough to home for you, ya cunt?' Patrick raised his voice and Michael backed down.

It was no good, Patrick was determined. He sent four boys out looking for his stolen car and phoned a contact in the force to see if they could trace the vehicle. Luckily for me I had a few hours head start and was about to change my mode of transportation again.

I'd abandoned the car in a layby outside Nottingham in a small village called Kimberley. I walked back to the motorway and in twenty minutes had hitched a lift with a lorry driver. An hour later he'd dropped me a couple of miles outside Leeds. I walked the last three miles or so through the dark and headed for the bright lights.

Forty minutes later I reached the city centre, the night's sky a circus tent of colour, the streets still busy with taxis and staggering bodies; ghosts swaying in and out of the sodium streetlamps, avoiding orange puddles upon the slabs. I quickly found a cheap bed and breakfast to spend the remainder of the night.

It was three in the morning but I couldn't sleep. I just kept going over and over the events of the day in my mind. I was a bundle of nerves – an edginess had infected my whole being. I wanted to lash out. I needed to sleep.

Willing things to be different, imagining all the scenarios that might have saved her. I eventually drifted off to sleep about five o'clock and woke to the sound of the trains screeching to a stop as they crossed the River Aire.

After calling in for breakfast at a greasy spoon I headed into the centre and the shops. I picked up a couple of things in the market; some pants and socks, a couple of t-shirts and a few toiletries. I also bought a new holdall to pack them in, dumped the old one in a bin and headed north on foot. I hitch-hiked to Bradford and then after an hour of thumbing I managed to get a lift across the moors to Kendal. I mulled over heading to Scotland but wasn't keen on the accents or the cold so just took a local bus to Penrith instead.

When I reached the small market town I explored the shops for a bit before looking around for holiday lets. I found a tiny cottage to rent a few miles from the start of the lakes in a place called Greystoke.

'It's a bijou residence with plenty of character,' said Raquel, the estate agent who was showing me around.

'Meaning I have to bow to get in?' I replied with a smile.

In ninety per cent of the bedroom I couldn't even stand up properly. Pouting Raquel shot me a few funny looks as I shuffled around the property, hunched over most of the time.

'How far is the nearest shop?' I asked.

'Oh less than five minutes, you do drive?'

'Yeh, I drive alright.'

Raquel showed me her perfect white teeth.

'Just don't have a car yet.'

'Ah... about two miles walk then,' she sighed thinking she'd now lost the sale.

'I'll take it.'

The Hollywood smile was back.

*

What the heck. It was cheap. It had also been painted recently although I guessed that was only to cover the damp.

For the first few days I endured a kind of sleep drought. In the morning I remember turning over and

116

over, screwing my eyes tight in search of a few more minutes rest. I'm a car crash, an emotional wreck.

I hardly eat for a week. I find myself alone and retreating into my memory. It's not a good place to be. On the bed in the afternoons I spend hours watching the clock, I draw my knees up to my chest and clasp my arms around them in a kind of foetal position. I miss her so much.

One night I found myself sat outside shivering. I'd been staring at the hills for hours. I'd fixated on a single sheep as it slowly and methodically progressed across the landscape stretched out before me. I was hungry and cold. I stood up in semi-darkness and went inside to cook eggs.

*

The chilly wind seems to fill the room even though I'd only left the window open a little. I'm lost. In a perpetual cycle of déjà vu. And for the first time in my life I'm afraid. Charley is gone and I'm next. I tried to shake the negative thoughts from my mind but they kept bouncing back like a demented yo-yo.

Girls weren't supposed to die like that. They solemnly held flowers in their laps. They wore black and cried at the graves of their men. Everything was back to front, upside down.

It was a moment that would stay with me forever. I wanted to rewind, play, edit... I needed to put it right, put it back together properly. Cut bits out. Swap them for nicer bits. Make it different. The way it should have been.

But I couldn't. There was nothing I could ever do that would make it alright.

Although I didn't plan to, I ended up spending a month there in that small house. And as each day passed so the hurt got worse not better. Time was not healing. All it did was gift me flashbacks and nightmares. I'd wake up in the middle of the night sweating, feeling sick or trembling.

When I did venture out, to pop to the local shop, get some supplies, a couple of magazines I just went straight back to the cottage. I did make a point of inspecting all the newspapers most days though. To check if there were any updates on the massacre down south, or if the police had any leads. But apart from a small piece I'd found in the Telegraph on the second day when I'd passed through Leeds, I found nothing else. Crazily, it never made the news, which just goes to show how much shit must have been happening in London back in the day.

*

'The name's Roy.'

'Steve,' I replied and held out my hand.

'Welsh are you?'

'Yeh, been abroad for the last ten years, doing a bit of travelling now. Looking for a job.'

'Buy me a pint and I might be able to help you laddie.'

Roy gave me his life story. Moving south from Scotland to find farm work he'd fallen in love with the landscape and a local girl. Forty years later he was still here although he'd been all alone since his wife died. He'd tended her at home until the cancer got too bad and in due course she moved into town and a hospice.

When I'd first spotted him at the bar I noticed his scruffy beard, threadbare cardigan and the string holding his trousers up. They say appearances can be deceptive.

'I need a bit of help on the old farm if you're interested? Odd jobs man you know.'

I bought him another beer. Then we went for a drive and he gave me a tour.

'All this?' I asked.

'Aye, all the way up to that peak in the distance.'

'Shit, how many acres is that?'

'Heh heh, too many laddie.'

Roy not only owned a holiday park but he also owned the farm that sat alongside it.

I volunteered to help, as long as I was allowed to stay on site. He nearly bit my arm off. Somehow I'd managed to find a safe hold up miles from anywhere with just this eccentric elderly man and one hundred sheep for company. I couldn't have found a better hideout if I'd tried.

Working during the day was fine. It took my mind off things. At night though, back in the van my anxiety returned. I became hypersensitive. So easily aroused and upset. I got stomach aches, I got annoyed with myself and struggled to concentrate on anything. I would sit by the window, can of beer in hand, portable TV talking to itself, crying to a god that obviously wasn't listening. Sometimes I'd be up all night. I watched the moon move across the sky. Stare for hours at the flurry of stars. Keep watching until I saw one fall. When it was really cold I swear I could see the ice painting a tapestry on the window.

Time slowed right down. Eventually I started to feel a bit better. I bought a pair of walking boots and started to stroll for hours around the country lanes and nearby villages, in between fixing up things around the campsite. I was soon as fit as a butcher's dog too, with not eating or drinking as much as usual. I lost about a stone in weight and started to look truly ripped as the heavy muscle toned down.

Occasionally I'd call in to a few pubs and have a glass of lager but as everyone knew everyone I decided it was best I didn't make a habit of it. I chatted to a few drinkers, told them I was on a rambling holiday and that I was on leave from the Marines, which they seemed to buy. If anyone asked what part of Wales I was from I simply said, "north", or Wrexham. No-one questioned the fact I sounded more like an Indian than a scouser. I tried to remember to add that I'd lived overseas for many years, which hopefully they'd remember to say if ever a trio of thickset Irishmen with big bulging overcoats happened to be passing through looking for their long-lost Welsh mate.

I liked the North of England, the people were friendly and the pace of life was certainly much slower than the big city. There wasn't much work apart from on the farms or in the tourist industry so I was thankful to get this job before I spent too much of my own money.

Six months later I went to say goodbye to Roy and his run-down caravan park.

'Hello?'

No answer.

'Roy? You home?'

I walked in to the farmhouse. Still silence.

My landlord was obviously out so I thought it best I leave. He never seemed comfortable on the few occasions I had been inside his home but then curiosity got the better of me. I opened a few cupboards to look for a biscuit or some other snack I could pinch for the road trip I was about to take.

'Fuckin hell!' I said out loud.

Roy apparently didn't like banks. I opened a couple more doors. There was cash everywhere, tons of it. I did a quick count and guessed there was at least fifty grand that I could see just in these few kitchen units.

What if he had more upstairs? Under the bed or floorboards?

It was very tempting but he'd been good to me and I didn't want to upset anyone else. I left him a note instead.

Time you visited the building society mate.

*

My breath caught in my throat as I jumped from a light sleep and dreams of the fairground at Christmas. Blue lights flickered outside the window and strobed the walls of my small bedroom. I was naked and quickly grabbed a pair of pants from the stone floor – like a cowboy snatching his boots. My pulse was racing as I slowly pulled the curtains apart to reveal an ambulance two doors up from my new digs.

I'd moved on again a few weeks back and found a small place to rent in Ambleside on the north of Lake Windermere. Visibly relaxing, I slumped back onto the bed and put my head in my hands. It was probably a feeble old git having a cardiac but when I saw the lights I assumed it was the police and they'd come for me.

I still had no idea what story had been spun about those fateful events back in London. I didn't know if they'd framed me somehow or had just done a runner and taken cover for a bit. Hopefully Patrick and his boys had more serious shit to attend to. He would either have to placate the Jamaicans or go full psycho killer on them. Half of me wished the darkies would get the upper hand but I knew that he wouldn't forget about me forever.

I wasn't thinking straight though. I even thought about going back to the city. I planned in meticulous detail how I would get close to him and how I'd do it. I wanted to beat him to a pulp and then watch the life leave him as I crushed his throat in my hands but on reflection a couple of bullets to his brain would be the more sensible approach.

I was still heartbroken but I knew I had to let her go. I wanted to kill Patrick more than anything but understood he'd be waiting. If I was being honest with myself I would never get near the bastard. And if I did manage to, it would more than likely be a one-way journey. They'd shoot me before I could get away. I had to move on with the mess that was my life and try to forget about revenge. There was an old saying I remembered about digging two graves anyway. Made sense.

By the time I left my room and ventured outside the late morning sun was pinpricking through the gaps in the foliage. The emergency services were gone and the road was calm again. Could I stay in Cumbria for good? I liked the hills a lot. Reminded me of Wales.

I contemplated planting a garden. I liked the smell of wet earth and flowers. I wanted to find a purpose in life. Something to make me feel better about myself.

Part of me was always running; part of me craved an end. Running faster towards tomorrow, a tomorrow that would arrive all too soon.

*

A month later I decided to travel again. It was becoming a habit now. The rent was a bit steep anyway so I decided to move further south. I'd become adept at living out of a suitcase, or rucksack to be more precise. My whole life could now be stuffed inside a forty-litre bag, which sat on my back as I wandered about the countryside. Once I'd found a spot to lay up for a bit I found myself going through the same routine. I'd relax for a few days, then count my money, before packing again, ready to flee at the slightest sign of trouble.

I'd found another job, a handyman on a caravan site near Penny Bridge and kept myself to myself. I walked a lot, ate healthier than I'd ever done in my life, cut down on the beer and joined a gym in Ulverston.

I remembered the mountains around my Welsh valley home, the light rolling in waves across the shades of green, the curve of the ancient oak and beech forests. They were great places to train for rugby. Pick a big hill and jog to the top. I hadn't spent enough time there though. My formative years were spent in alleyways and pubs not fields and open spaces. There was little room for gentleness in my life. My entire existence had been jagged, jumbled and uneven. Until Charley...

*

I was allowed to borrow a car from the campsite, a rundown, black Ford Escort that got me around, and what I reasoned might turn into a year ended up being five. I settled in to the outdoor life and almost felt content again. Almost.

When I was busy it was fine but whenever I had a few days off the guilt would still hit me like a train. I still replayed that fateful afternoon over and over. It was like an itch you couldn't scratch, a dream where you were screaming but nobody heard you. Running to stand still.

Then for no reason it happened again. I woke up one day to the clock ticking loud next to my ear and I knew I had to move on. I had always realised that my size and Welsh accent made me stand out a fair bit so maybe it wasn't such a good idea to hang around anywhere longer than necessary. But it had been years now. Years of relative calm.

Maybe they'd forgotten about me? How could I tell though? As conspicuous as I was I imagined that Michael and the gang would also stand out like a pork chop in a synagogue so I'd hopefully get a bit of advance warning if they did show up asking questions. I still couldn't relax though. Perhaps I'd never be free. Always looking over my shoulder. It wasn't a good feeling to wake up with or a great one to fall asleep to.

It wasn't the best plan I ever came up with but I decided enough time had elapsed to risk it. I'd go home. Back to the land of my father. The father who was god knows where.

Twenty

I got the train from Cumbria to Liverpool but the home of The Beatles was no good because the people were far too friendly. Everyone wanted to know who you were, where you'd come from, what you were doing and so on... There were a lot of Irish too. After a week of being a tourist that stood out like a sore thumb I left.

Catching a bus down to north Wales I tried Prestatyn first, before leaving after a few weeks to head to Rhyl. It wasn't much of an improvement but I felt more comfortable being on the move. The town was the birthplace of Ruth Ellis, an escort who was the last woman to be hanged in Britain after she put four bullets from a revolver into her lover in 1955. That should have given me a hint.

Broken glass crunched under my boots as I wandered about the seafront looking for a room. The place was awash with dilapidated bed and breakfasts, small, handwritten signs in every window. Every other property was filled with low-life benefit scroungers from Merseyside, just about all of them hooked on hard drugs.

Finding a one-bedroom bedsit I resigned myself to another extended period of mundane routine – find a job and do a bit of training until the restlessness returned. I was getting used to the feelings now. Waking up each morning I asked myself if I had any reason to get out of bed. I couldn't actually settle anywhere. My whole life was turning into a visit.

'Cheer up mate, it might never happen?'

'What?'

'You look like you've found a penny but lost a pound mate?'

'I'm not your mate,' I said.

'OK, sorry, just making conversation.'

I raised my hand in apology but didn't look up from my beer.

It wasn't the best time to be in north Wales. There weren't many jobs to be had, especially if I wanted to keep myself below the radar. Crime was rife and the pubs' regulars weren't particularly sociable either. Plus it was difficult to find a true local in amongst the huge influx of transients.

'British seaside resorts like Rhyl were glamorous holiday destinations one time,' continued Rob, an old Dudley Arms regular.

I finally gave in.

'Think I must have missed that era mate,' I grinned.

'Aye, natural beauty and carefree nightlife,' added my new best friend as he swung his arm in a semi-circle for effect.

I bought him a pint and we did the usual introductions. I was a welder named Chris, looking for work.

'What happened here? It's just boarded up shops and businesses now eh?'

'Yeh, it's definitely gone to the dogs these days.'

'Think you're over-selling it a bit there Rob.'

He laughed and nodded his head.

*

Rhyl at the time was one of the poorest places I'd ever seen. It was plagued by heroin and notorious for having one of the highest death rates from drug overdoses in the UK. It was 1996 and this was the "Trainspotting" generation in action in sleepy Wales.

The decline probably started in the sixties but got worse as the decades slipped by. Another consequence of these sink towns was that drug deaths increased in the over forty-age group as opposed to the usual twenty and thirty-year olds. The legacy of the Tory policy to divide and conquer, leaving the hapless and hopeless to scrounge around for the scraps thrown to them by those lucky enough to have been dealt a better hand in life's sick poker game.

Around this time about half of all drug-related deaths were from similar UK holiday towns. Places like Blackpool, Bournemouth, Hastings and Portsmouth were high on the list but towns I knew well, like Port Talbot and Swansea down south and the whole of the north coast, where I ended up bumming around for about a year, were also up there.

Why I stayed in such a depressing, soul-destroying place I have no idea. Was just being in Wales enough to satisfy me at that time? Maybe, even though it was mostly the English immigrants that were responsible for the flood of product and the violent crime that accompanied the business.

I got a few odd jobs to tide me over and bought a car, a beat up old Toyota Corolla. During that year I often toyed with the idea of leaving, heading south, maybe to Brecon or even home to the valleys but after a small incident in a rundown pub on the main street of Rhyl I knew it best I go walkabout again first. Just in case word got back to London about a big Welsh lad throwing his weight around.

You wouldn't think anyone could get into too much trouble, leaning on the bar one quiet Tuesday afternoon, in an empty pub, in a shitty coastal community in the arse of the world. Wrong!

If I'd knocked back my half of lager about two minutes faster I would have been strolling to the chip shop, oblivious to the activities of pan-European crime lords but synchronicity is a funny old thing.

'Oi, cunt. Fuck off,' said the skeletal prick that had just walked in like he owned the place.

'I beg your pardon sir?' I replied, happy for some conversation no matter how limited in intellectual stimulation it might be.

'You not hear pal, get out now before I throw you out.'

I rose slowly from my stool. Where would his blade be hiding? No-one can be this stupid.

My sixteen and a half stone, inverted triangular shape that bulged through my skin-tight t-shirt was still not registering correctly on this little toe-rag so I decided to wind him up a bit more and smiled in his general direction. Wankers like this hated that. It showed a lack of respect and it would mean he'd be forced to make the first move in order to defend his honour, even though the barman was the only other witness and he didn't seem to give a flying fuck. Probably seen it all before.

He moved fast, I'll give him that and as he

approached I saw his arm quickly reach behind his shirt. Obviously going for the weapon tucked into the back of his jeans. He didn't quite make it though as I hit him hard under his chin with the bottom of my palm. I followed up by kicking him across the carpet and then jumped on his head with both feet. His nose broke, a couple of teeth fell out and I heard a low moan emanate from his prone body as he slowly moved into a foetus-like bundle on the floor.

Should I go back to the bar for another drink? Seeing large shadows pass the misted windows of the front room I opted for a change of scenery. I opened the door just as the two figures were about to do the same. The one bloke was an old-school tough guy, your stereotypical, thickset bagman or minder type, the other guy was shorter, foreign-looking, middle-eastern or something.

I smiled an excuse me and managed to quickly sneak past them before they walked inside. I jogged around the corner and into the next boozer before they realised their local contact, a low-life pusher was still crawling on the Axminster looking for the tooth fairy and trying to work out how a buffalo had been allowed in the bar.

'You okay Dai?' asked Scott the barman of The Swan Inn.

'Aye mate, just a spot of disco-dancing next door.'

'Oh shit. Lucky escape I'd say.'

'Why's that?'

'I don't know his name but rumour is a well-known Liverpool gangster is in town.'

'Go on...'

'Well, he's meeting a Turkish drug lord or something. You don't want to mess with them...'

'Marvellous.'

It was yet another lucky escape. It seemed everybody in town knew except me. Time to move on and find somewhere quieter again.

*

Not wanting to be hiding all my life I decided I'd risk some exposure, if only to get a bit more cash behind me. I started working in a few nightclubs along the coast. I drove between Flint and Colwyn Bay and took whatever shitty job I could find.

I started taking mental notes, learning the dealers' faces, seeing how much they made. I had no problem stealing from these dirt bags but decided it best if I allowed myself to be bribed a little. It looked better that way. I worked all hours and saved every penny for the next few months.

It was Christmas Day and I was ambling along the shoreline. It was freezing cold and a gale was howling over the Irish Sea. The electricity from the grey sky seemed to awaken my hangover. I'd allowed myself a few lagers last night.

I worked for two more weeks and by the New Year I had another few grand stashed away. Time to go walkies.

Twenty One

I left the bad weather behind as I parked the Toyota next to the train station at Llanfairfechan. In the distance I watched the rain as it swirled around the majestic Gylder mountains. The wind dropped as I crossed the river and headed for the deserted beach. Stumbling over the rocks I soon got to the sand and immediately felt the icy chill of the sea as the wind hit me. The straw-coloured sunshine of the late afternoon was slowly fading and I knew it would be getting even colder soon. It was best I found somewhere with a duvet.

I popped into a café near the front, picked up a can of Lilt and walked to the desk where a nice-looking, young girl sat staring out into space and blowing bubbles with her chewing gum.

'Hi love, any ideas where I can find a room in town?' I asked.

'Be' am drio un o'r tafarndau yn y dref?' came the reply through pink teeth.

'Okay, ta... diolch,' I stuttered back and after paying for my drink wandered back towards the centre to look for a pub with a bed.

At that time I had no idea if I was going to stay but knew that this place was a far better option to lay low than the skank-filled, bedsit towns further along the north coast. Less criminals, less scousers and less chance of me getting into trouble that might attract unwanted attention.

A few months later I was starting to feel like a local. In reality it was more like a few days seeing as the local community was so small. I'd managed to find a labouring job on a local farm and the old man seemed to like having me around so he could practice his English on someone from down south. Although I'd never planned to stay that long, the weeks and months slowly clocked up and it was nice to be away from the degradation of towns like Abergele and Rhyl.

Eventually I got bored, as I knew I would, and decided it was time to split. I spent a nice summer down the Llyn peninsular, just bumming around really, before stopping again in Aberystwyth, or "Aber" as it was known to one and all.

Another Welsh speaking area, which I didn't mind, as it was just as easy for me to spot a stranger in town as the locals to suss me as one. The following spring moving into summer saw the place get overrun with brummies on holidays, but again this was fine with me. As long as I didn't hear a cockney or Irish accent I was happy to simply go with the flow. I found the odd job here and there, a bit of bouncing work and went for plenty of walks along the famous front as well as up into the woods, following the River Rheidol inland from the town.

*

A year or so later and I was back on the road. The motorway was deathly quiet. A single orange flame was shooting high into the night sky.

I had a vision of it burning non-stop for the last thirty years, maybe longer. It certainly seemed that way. It reached up into the blackness, polluting the stars. The surreal landscape was part apocalyptic horror, part fairground attraction. I passed Port Talbot about midnight.

From a distance the flat, seaside town seemed quaint, nestling innocently beneath the convex mountainside that towered above, but as you approached closer the maze of pipe works and harsh metal structures became illuminated by a hundred white lights that were dotted all over the sprawling site.

During its peak in the 1960s, the Abbey Works was the biggest steelworks in Europe and employed eighteen thousand people, making it the largest employer in south Wales. It was nationalised in 1967 and absorbed into British Steel.

I checked the rear view mirror through puffy eyes as I drove at exactly fifty miles an hour down the M4. Happy to have left Swansea behind I needed to make a decision soon. If I kept driving I'd be in Cardiff in an hour and a sitting duck if anyone from London recognised me and reported back to Patrick.

The sky grew darker as the lights behind me disappeared. I decided to take the next exit.

Between my legs I still had a bottle of energy drink and the wrappers of long-eaten chocolate bars lay on the passenger seat. On the floor were three empty coffee cartons. It had been a long drive but I'd made good time with so little traffic on the roads of west Wales at this time.

The only headlights I saw now were from huge lorries slowly trudging their way to Swansea docks or further west to Fishguard and the ferry to Ireland. My eyes suddenly felt heavy. My head was overcome with an anaesthetic haze. A foggy, blocked-ears feeling of vertigo. I needed to rest. To sleep.

Where the hell was I heading? I certainly never thought I'd settle in one place ever again. Charley had said life happens when you're making other plans. She was about to be proved right.

I saw the sign for Porthcawl and indicated left as a thousand, imagined happy childhood memories came flooding back. I remembered staying in a caravan with mam and dad when I was about eight or nine years old. "Costa del Trecco" dad used to call it. Then I recalled him slapping my mam across the face to stop her screaming at him and the tears started to roll down my cheeks as I slowed the car down to take the slip road exit.

Twenty Two

1999

I was woken by the first rays of sunlight as they crept into the car through the steamed up windows. I was freezing to my bones and starving. My warm morning breath came out in white clouds.

I'd pulled over a few miles outside of town and parked in a partly hidden layby to get five minutes rest. I'd slept for about three or four hours instead. I started the car and cruised slowly down to town passing bright verdant fields as I went. Cream-coloured sheep were strewn around the emerald baize meadows. I passed the dilapidated old fairground of Coney Island, a romantic name, which conjured up images of a vibrant New York boardwalk but unfortunately the reality was far from that.

Situated on a low limestone headland on the Glamorganshire coast the seaside town of Porthcawl had been one of the premier holiday destinations in south Wales since agriculture and industry declined around 1900, although the nearby village of Newton dated as far back as the 12th Century. The church, come fortress, was founded by knights from Jerusalem apparently.

I smelt the salt coming off the sea and followed the road to the marina as it curved to the right and joined the Esplanade, a promenade built in 1887 to commemorate Queen Victoria's Golden Jubilee. As I approached the Grand Pavilion I turned inland onto Mary Street to look for some digs.

Parking up about half way down I noticed a

nondescript bed and breakfast that had seen better days but looked perfect for my needs.

'Okay I can knock off a bit if you're staying longer,' said the gangly landlady.

I had to stop myself laughing at her down at heel slippers and laddered tights.

'Great, thanks.'

She seemed delighted that anyone would be interested in taking a room at this time of year and practically snatched my hand off as I held out a few notes to pay for a week in advance.

'No funny business though. This is a respectable house.'

I watched the smoke rise from her Embassy. Reminded me of the refinery towers back west.

'Just looking for somewhere peaceful to while away a bit of time,' I said.

'I have a garage if you need one,' she offered.

I took a stroll down to the shops and picked up a few beers and some snacks. My room was small but clean and I could see myself staying here for as long as it took me to get restless again.

Dragging a chair to the window I cracked the ring pull on a can and sipped McEwan's lager for breakfast as I watched the seagulls fighting outside in the street. It had been eight years since I'd run away from London. Eight years since Charley had been killed and not a day had gone by when I didn't relive those horrific few seconds.

Sometimes I'd go a few days without dwelling on it too much and occasionally I'd think about the good times we shared in Cardiff, the crazy things I'd got up to before we met up again. I even had fond memories of the laughs I had with Michael and the boys.

I thought about little Morgan, hoped she was doing alright, and not spending too much time with that bastard of a father, Patrick. Then the red mist would return and I'd want to see him again. One on one. Just me and him and no weapons. I'd take great pleasure in beating him senseless. He was a tough one but I'd take him, no question. I was thirty-six and in the prime of my life, physically anyway. Yeh, maybe I'd consider looking him up?

Being back in Wales had certainly affected me. I was starting to feel more confident. Was I finally free? Free from the constant looking over the shoulder and wondering if the walk to the shop, the stroll on the beach or the pint in the local would be the last thing I'd ever do before the blackness came.

'Come on, snap out of it twat.' I said out loud.

I smiled to myself. I'd always liked Porthcawl. It was a nice town.

Peaceful.

Nothing could go wrong here…

Twenty Three

2000

She eyed me like she was watching a shooting star for the first time. She was grey and unwashed, and wore a large beige overcoat with a fake fur collar. Unfastened buttons showed off the goods underneath. A nice, round pair of small tits were kept in place by a tight, black crop top that invited me closer. Her skin was blanched like driftwood, her pierced bellybutton was inflamed and sore, and discoloured, bloated legs stuck out from under a short, red plastic skirt.

'Looking for business love?' she blurted out, even though it was still light and we were stood only a few yards from the harbour front.

'No, sorry love, I was just waiting for someone.'

'Aye? Your wife is it?' she chuckled, seeing I was uneasy and now fidgeting from one foot to the next.

She looked freezing cold and I instantly felt sorry for her, even though I knew she would rob me as good as look at me.

'Can I buy you a coffee?' I asked.

'Aye, alright love.'

*

In the first few weeks I'd made myself a regular at a back table in Sidoli's café on the corner of John Street. From my vantage point I could see everyone who walked in and was also just a few yards away from slipping out the back door if necessary. Old habits die hard. I took her there.

'What's your name love?' I asked the young girl who was now sat opposite me.

'Whatever you want it to be,' she replied with a grin but I could see it was bravado. I just stared.

'Oh okay then. Kate. But everyone calls me Kat.'

'Hi Kat, I'm Paul.'

She ran her hands through her shoulder length, jet-black hair. Teasing the curls back into position.

'Please tell me you weren't really doing what I think you were doing?' I ask.

'Well, a girl has to make a living don't she?'

'Not that way she don't,' I scolded, noticing red marks on her forearms as she raised the coffee cup to her lips.

She reminded me of the androgynous-looking girls I'd seen in London. You'd pass them one day and they seemed fine. Scruffy yeh, but happy enough. Some might even say cool. Like they knew something I didn't. Then as the weeks rolled by you'd see a change. The ones you still recognised would take on this faraway look, and then it got worse.

They might have thought they could handle it but the truth is far from that. So many youngsters imagined they'd hang out for a few years, enjoy themselves. Live life to the full, then pack it in and head off to University or a decent job but it didn't work out like that. Most ended up living from one fix to the next.

One of the doormen back in Cardiff had told me once that drugs were like a plane crash. They don't differentiate. It doesn't matter if you're in first class or economy. When the aircraft's going down, so are you.

Kat and I chatted for an hour and I bought her chips, which she covered in six big squirts of tomato sauce, before moving them around her plate without eating more than two or three.

'I better get going, thanks for the drink,' said Kat, jumping to her feet quickly and almost tipping the table over. She started to look jumpy and I guessed right that she most likely needed a hit of something.

'Where do you live?' I asked.

'Esplanade Avenue, bedsit. It's a fuckin' shit hole. Do you want to come back?'

'How can a guy refuse an offer like that?'

'Well?'

'I can walk you there if you want,' I offered. It was early evening and the café was closing anyway and I didn't have anything better to do.

'I didn't even like heroin to begin with,' Kat confessed on the brief walk around the corner to her place. 'It was a sort of birthday present from an ex-boyfriend. I was eighteen and it seemed like a laugh. That was six or seven years ago now.'

'Thoughtful present...'

'Woz ah?'

'Sorry to hear that, I said. Can't you give it up?' I asked.

Kat laughed. 'I had a job, only bar work but it was enough to pay the bills and I used to deal a bit to afford my own habit. I was coping alright until they caught me pinching from the till and I got sacked. That was a couple of years back and that was when I started on the game

141

like.'

'I'm not a fan of drugs. Never have been. Why don't you just quit? Can't you get treatment? Go to the doctors, get off it in hospital or something?'

'Havin' a laugh are you? Well, I tried that once but once you're out again what can you do eh? I was straight back on it. You mix with the same people and with no work what choice did I have? They reckon there's about half a million addicts in the UK now and only a tenth of them are having treatment. It's shit.'

I'd picked a couple of cans up in the local shop on the way and we drank them in Kat's bedsit. I notice under the harsh fluorescent lighting she has in her room that she's even more weathered than I'd initially thought. She's painfully thin and although she still has all her teeth, her gums are receding and a few teeth have started to go slightly black at the edges.

Kat walked to the filthy window and stood with her back to me. Dusk had descended and blotted out the view. It appeared to be raining but it was hard to tell through the grey murkiness. Rooftops opposite hovered, like ghosts in the thick air.

She darted across the room to the light switch. Darkness didn't help disguise the smell of mildew or the shabbiness of the room. On a bookshelf near where she sits down there is a trashy, dog-eared paperback. Just the one.

'Not much of a library?' I ask, pointing to the empty shelf.

'I can give you a handjob for a tenner?' she smiled seductively.

'Fuckin' hell love, no. Where did that come from?' I took out thirty quid and placed it in her palm. Her face lit up.

She went to speak but I interrupted. 'Don't you want to stop?'

'Yeh, course I fuckin' do. Thanks for the money.' Kat seemed embarrassed and looked away from me.

She then proceeds to give me a lecture on the whole scene.

'I'm only twenty-five but I know I look twice that.'

I don't contradict her and she doesn't care.

'I spend the days getting high but I also buy some extra brown and sell it on for a profit. You wouldn't believe who buys this shit. My regulars include shop workers, teachers, and even a nurse. You'd think she'd know better yeh?'

'Go on,' I encourage her, intrigued to hear about things from the users side rather than the side I'd known in previous years.

'Normal people, like you,' she points a bony, accusing finger at me. 'With normal jobs and stuff. They can be functioning addicts you know. They go to work and just use for recreation. They buy off me on their way home to their kids mun. Mad innit?'

Kat proceeds to tell me about how much power the drug has over her.

'You'll sleep with anyone for a few quid. As long as you have enough for the next fix. Even you would,' she shoots me an icy look.

'What do you mean? I'd never do something I didn't want to love.'

'Wanna bet? You'd let benders shag you up the arse in Merthyr Mawr for a quarter of a gram.'

'If you say so, but I'd probably strangle them afterwards,' I laughed.

Kat was sizing me up again. I got the impression that everything was a hustle to her. Nothing could be taken at face value. Her entire existence was a negotiation.

The carpet was tattered, stained and dirty. I didn't know why I'd gone back there. It suddenly seemed like a bad idea. I craved fresh air, the feel of cold drizzle on my skin again.

'Do you want to try some?'

'No ta love. I'm not looking for a magic carpet ride. Got enough shit to deal with without complicating it with chemicals.'

I got up and walked out. A wave of nausea rushing over me.

'See you again.'

Twenty Four

The sky was murky and blue; bruised purple like a wound. The grey clouds drifted aimlessly across the bay towards the breakwater and the old, cast iron, gas lighthouse that had only been converted to electric two years earlier. I sat down and stared out to sea for fifteen minutes. I watched a fishing boat slowly bob across the hem of the jumpy horizon.

Catching sight of her my spirits rose for a second. At least I knew someone to talk to. It was a kind of belonging. Not the same *hiraeth* as the valleys where everyone knew everyone but it was a start. She shambled across the big bend in the road, ignoring a car that tooted her, fag in hand and a supermarket bag dragging behind her. She looked a mess.

We'd been seeing each other regularly since that first chance meeting. Not in a romantic sense, just as friends. I had plenty of time on my hands and apart from running on the beach and a spot of weight training I was a free man. I took it on myself to do some good in the world. Kat would be my penance.

'So tell me what it's like?' I said, as I watched her push a needle into a vein on the back of her hand. She ignores me as her face becomes flushed and in a few seconds Kat starts scratching her head, and then lays down on the bed. Her eyes roll back in her skull and I can tell she's feeling it already. Straight to the liver, then the brain's pleasure receptors.

'How do you feel?' I ask.

'Warm,' she smiles. 'And tingly.'

Her head lolls to the side and she falls forward onto the sheets. Her whole body becomes wilted, she goes limp and looks as content as a baby in its mother's loving embrace.

I continued to watch as Kat seemed to sleep, although I knew by now that she was just savouring the moment. When a user injects, as opposed to smokes heroin, they get addicted faster and develop tolerance sooner. She would be in bliss for half an hour, then feel normal for the rest of the day but then need another shot before bedtime.

The amount of money she got through was staggering. Should I take out the dealer she got her stuff from? That would be easy enough. Trouble was he'd come back with a gang of mates with knives and baseball bats. Even if I managed to survive that there'd be others. It wouldn't end well.

On the plus side it appeared what she bought wasn't too impure. Often at street level, dealers would cut the drug with other substances to increase their profit margins. They often mixed in sugar, starch, quinine and even the deadly alkaloid strychnine!

I had tried to take her mind off it, taken her for walks, bought her food, a few drinks in the pub, we even took a stroll around the local library where I pointed out a couple of good books for her to get into. I was a big reader back in those days. Nothing worked though.

For most of the day she was fine, just a normal girl. Then I'd notice her mood change. She'd start itching. She'd get restless. Not just a bit fidgety but big time twitchy. Sometimes she'd bend over in pain as a muscle spasm or stomach cramp would hit her.

'How about going cold turkey?' I suggested, one night.

'No, it's horrible.'

'Have you ever tried?'

'Yeh, but it can kill you.'

'That's not what I've heard. Alcoholics can die 'cos they react badly to withdrawal. I don't think it's as bad for brown.'

'Okay, I'll try. As long as you stay with me.'

For two days I watched Kat experience convulsions and sickness. She'd tell me she wanted to die, she worried about the slightest thing. I tried to comfort her but it was no good.

On the third day we were sat in her flat. I held her close to me while she sobbed into my shoulder. She stayed there for an hour and I felt her heart beating faster as she sweated into my clothes. Then abruptly she forced me away and ran to the toilet and threw up everywhere. I helped her to her feet and she literally begged me for a hit. I gave in, pushover that I'd become.

We went for a walk and she found her dealer at the Rock Hotel. I watched as she handed him a few notes and he smirked at me. My mind instantly shot back to Charley. I wanted to kill him. What was the point of people like him anyway? The planet didn't need them. People like Patrick. People like me...

I felt it was my duty to make him pay for the mess he'd made of Kat's life. Pure hate rose quickly inside me and it took all my reserve to stop myself heading over to where he leaned on the end of the bar and pushing a glass through his skull until it came out the other side.

Back in the flat Kat is much happier. I watch fascinated as she goes through her usual ritual. Everything done in the same way, the same order with the same paraphernalia.

Heroin comes in powdered form and must be melted before being injected. Kat would empty the little bag, mix the powder with water, then add a few squirts of lemon juice from a Jif bottle. She had a favourite spoon, which was black with soot from her favourite lighter. The one she used to heat the liquid.

If she had cotton wool she used that to absorb the liquid before drawing it up into the syringe. The cotton wool helped to filter out impurities apparently.

I had never felt so helpless as I did when I watched her routine. I wanted to lash out, to kick the needle out of her hand to tell her it would be alright, that she'd be okay tomorrow. I knew she wouldn't though.

'I'm fine,' she said, trying to reassure me.

'No, you're not,' I reply. 'This stuff is evil. Nothing good will ever come of this. It will kill you.'

'I know,' she smiled back, like a lost child in the dark woods.

I knew then this couldn't go on.

Twenty Five

By 2002 the M4 motorway that ran through south Wales was affectionately known as the crack highway, and while Cardiff, Newport and Swansea were all awash with crack, mostly supplied by Jamaican gangsters, heroin was still the drug of choice for many. Kat was pretty much hooked on heroin but had not progressed to crack. Yet.

I was curled up in bed one morning, sleeping off a few beers from the night before when she hammered a scabbed fist on the door. She was screaming for cash. I hadn't seen her for a few days. I needed some space away from her chaotic existence. The constant round of calls on fellow addicts, the wandering up and down John Street and arranging to meet up with, and I use the word loosely, friends.

'Okay, hang on, I'm coming.'

I opened the door. Kat looked like death warmed up; sunken eyes, ashen skin and seemed to have lost weight since I'd last seen her.

'You hungry?' I asked.

'Yeh, starving.' A welcome change.

I pulled on my shorts and a t-shirt and we strolled to the promenade. The autumn sun was low in the sky but I didn't need a jacket. The darkening clouds still held more rain and out to sea a rainbow faded in and out of sight as an oil tanker slowly crawled across the line between sea and skyline.

After leaving the kiosk on the front and quickly devouring the ice creams I'd bought we head into the town, just a street over and into Sidoli's café.

I order a large all-day breakfast with chips and a pot of tea. Kat orders a coffee and a plate of chips. I unfold my newspaper and skim through the back pages, annoyed by the amount of football coverage and seek out the biased English rugby section before reading the small column about the Welsh team at the bottom.

'I've made a decision,' she blurts out.

'Yes, pray tell,' I folded the paper in half and set it down next to me.

'You've got egg on your cheek.'

'Oh sorry, go on then, what have you decided?'

'I wanna get clean Paul. Will you help me?'

I'd read that addicts need a number of things to kick the habit and I'd just heard the most important one straight from the horse's mouth as it were. She wanted to.

'Aye course I will love.'

*

'Look doc, she needs it on prescription,' I said, on Kat's behalf.

'Okay, I'll see what we can do. Are you her father?'

I had to quickly stop myself telling the quack to go forth and multiply. Did I look that old? Jesus!

There were interviews and appointments. Eventually she got the meds. I remember waiting in the chemist one time. We watched and waited in morbid anticipation as the pharmacist poured liquids and shook bottles to mix the sediment up. Then they typed up notes and finally called Kat's name.

They watched as she downed the drug. Kat told

150

me what a great feeling it was to walk out of there, one more day over. One more day closer to redemption.

'It's like the whole world is mine,' she said.

'Wha' da ya mean?'

'I hate them looking. Like they're judging me and stuff. But when I knock it back I'm free again. Free for another day. I need a hot chocolate.'

Kat liked a warm drink afterwards. She said it helped wash the syrupy taste away, made the meds rush into the system faster and the small high came quicker too.

We popped into a coffee shop. We now had a café ritual each day as well.

*

A couple of weeks later Kat was in agony. Methadone is not great. It affects different people in different ways. As the dose is reduced so the withdrawal symptoms begin, like the dreaded stomach cramps.

With Kat she started to drink milk, lots of it. Then she wanted Jelly Babies, I was on Spar duty to satisfy her cravings. She slept better though, sometimes for twelve hours straight.

She had been constipated for four days when one morning she jumped out of bed and ran to the bathroom. I straightened up in the chair I was dozing in. Initially I was concerned but it soon became apparent what the problem was.

'Fuckin' hell babe, you stink! You given birth to an alien in there?'

The door opened a few minutes later. Kat was laughing. Real giggles. It was a breakthrough of sorts.

*

Three months later and she was doing good. Every fortnight she had a check-up. They took bloods and everyone could see the change in the girl. She'd blossomed into an attractive woman. I bought her little presents every time she did something good, nothing much, just a new top to wear or a sit-down meal in one of the pubs in town. She wasn't high maintenance, just grateful someone treated her as a human being instead of a low-life skank, which in fairness, she had been.

'Do you think I might be able to go to college?' asked Kat.

'Yeh, don't see why not. There's one in Bridgend isn't there?'

'I don't want to go there.'

'Why not?'

'Well, let me see now...'

I knew it was coming, I'd missed something. This young woman was sharp alright.

'Oh hi love, how are you? Didn't I take you down the dunes for a fuck last year? Oh yeh mister lecturer sir, so you did. Sker beach wasn't it? We walked past the plaque in memory of the forty-seven sailors who went down with the S.S. Santampa and then I went down on...'

'Alright I get it. Sorry.'

She watched me with a docile expression.

'Right, so what would you study?' I ask, trying to

change the subject.

'Dunno. Hairdressing maybe? Loads of money in that. All cash in hand too.'

It was good she was thinking this way. That she thought she was employable again. She seemed excited about life rather than fearful of it.

I couldn't help notice Kat's curly dark hair was starting to look healthier than when I'd first laid eyes on her. She had begun to wear a little makeup too. Like she was trying to impress someone perhaps.

'Okay, so what you up to tonight?' I asked.

'New Year's Eve aye mun. You asking me out Paul?' she joked with me.

'No... Well maybe a couple of drinks, that's all? We can celebrate you getting clean by pouring tons of alcohol into your system.'

'Oi, that's not very nice. I have an addictive personality I do.'

Later that night we went out to a bar overlooking the esplanade for a few, then played a few tunes on the jukebox in the Pier. Kat stuck fifty pence in the slot and the dulcet tones of Half Man Half Biscuit belted out The Trumpton Riots.

'So romantic,' I said.

My choice was slightly more mellow, Fire and Rain by James Taylor.

'What shit is this?' asked Kat.

'Quality love, you wouldn't know anything about that though.'

'Aye, that's why I'm with you is it?' she giggled.

Twenty Six

When we'd first become friends I had tended to keep my old life a secret. I didn't want to bore Kat with stories of my former existence and although it had been years since I'd fled London I still had to be careful. So in the early days I never invited her back to my place but just hung around her bedsit instead.

As the treatment seemed to be working and she'd been clean for a while I decided it was safe to go back to Cardiff and also take a quick recce up the valleys to see what the latest gossip was. Not that I imagined for a minute anything that new or exciting had happened. It never did.

*

Back in Porthcawl I took a few of my old clothes out of the suitcase and then pushed it under the bed. I had a few personal effects left in there, including a couple of photographs of Charley. I toyed with the idea of getting the best one framed but then thought better of it. It would just depress me. Having a daily reminder of how happy I used to be was not a great plan. I found a few old cassette tapes in there too. Dylan, the Stones, Jefferson Airplane and a couple of Johnny Cash albums.

'Who the fuck is he?' Kat was holding an old album up.

'The man in black love.'

'Looks like Elvis. You a teddy boy? I draw the line at that.'

'No, it's country…'

'Oh fuck no, even worse!'

I had weird taste apparently.

Although I was never one for technology even I knew it was time I got with the programme a bit. I gathered up my music and threw them all straight in the bin.

'Aw, don't do that, I'm sorry, I was only kidding like.'

'No, it's not you Kat.'

'You sure big boy?'

'Aye, honest. Must start looking for a nice CD player though.'

Twenty Seven

2004

The winter seemed to fly by and soon I was back in my favourite uniform – shorts and t-shirt – as summer approached. I was eating well, had given up the drink and junk food, and was also going to the gym four or five times a week. My biceps were over seventeen inches, my six-pack was back and I was in high spirits. Kat was looking good too, she had been clean for about two years and had filled out a bit as well. We saw each other most days and more or less every weekend.

She'd asked me to come back home with her a few times and made it crystal clear what she wanted by rubbing her hands all over my chest, arse and legs but I always declined, putting her amorous attention down to too much watermelon Bacardi Breezer or Diamond White.

Although I was in the prime of my life, being eleven years older than Kat, I always considered myself an old fart and thought she deserved better than a bum like me. I should have recognised the way she looked at me though. Only one other person had stared at me that way and she was buried in a north London cemetery.

*

It was the last week of July and the valley heads were in town, partying big time – the only way we knew how. It was the regular two-week factory shutdown, or miners' fortnight as it was still called, even though Thatcher had succeeded in closing most of the pits years earlier. The famous holiday overlapped the end of one month and the beginning of the next.

Historically, Porthcawl had always had pretensions of being a tourist watering hole even after the decline of industry in south Wales. A pleasant sea-facing walkway, plenty of pubs and chip shops, not to mention the seven beaches meant it was still popular, especially with the valley folk.

By the seventies and eighties the old charabancs of Dylan Thomas' days had been replaced by Vauxhall Cavaliers and caravans at Trecco Bay and Happy Valley. And although the mass exodus of virtually the whole population of the valley's towns and villages to Porthcawl had trickled off as cheap flights to Spain offered more sun, sex and sangria than an overcast, British seaside resort could provide there were still thousands of holidaymakers who still came to the coast.

On the edge of town, a few yards behind Coney beach was the funfair. And for two weeks the hard-earned cash from hundreds of working class families, that definitely couldn't afford it, was spent willingly. Gobbled up by donut sellers, ice cream parlours, penny arcades and the famous Water Shute ride.

I remembered coming to the beach as a child and although Kat wanted to hide from the crowds, a sense of nostalgia must have kicked in because I insisted we go to town one sunny afternoon.

We spent a few quid in the arcades and then grabbed a cornet before going for a walk on the beach.

'You're just a big kid aren't you?' accused Kat.

'No I'm not. It's a nice day and it'd be a shame to stay indoors,' I lied.

'Fancy a drink then?'

'Given up haven't I mun.'

'Afraid you can't keep up with a girl?' she teased.

'Okay, what the hell, it's not like I'm an alkie is it…' I stopped myself.

'Sorry,' I said. 'I didn't mean to…'

'It's fine Paul, I'm alright, seriously.'

We had a few ciders in the General Picton, followed by a stroll to the Rock Hotel. The sun and the beer soon went to my head and I was struggling to keep up with Kat who was pushing the pace and giving me sly, wicked winks, in between grabbing handfuls of my thigh.

By the time we staggered back to my flat I was pretty wrecked and incapable of talking, no matter anything more romantic. We crashed out until morning when I felt her slide out of bed and head to the bathroom. I turned over and tried to will my bladder to shrink because I didn't want to leave the safety of my warm sheets.

When I eventually gave in to the sensation in my groin and went for a wee I had to step over Kat who was sat cross-legged on the floor with my suitcase open and my scant possessions scattered over the carpet.

'Who's she?' she demanded, holding up a photo of Charley.

I snapped. 'Nobody, put it away!'

'Girlfriend, wife?'

'None of your fuckin' business.'

'Oh yeh, hit a nerve have I?'

'You have no idea, put them away, get your clothes on and piss off.'

Happy holidays. Kat dressed quickly, her eyes daggers, she slammed the front door behind her.

'Shit, shit, shit!' I cursed out loud, then rolled over and tried to fall back to sleep.

*

I didn't bother calling round to see Kat for a week or so. I'd put the snaps away and thought no more of it but when we did bump into each other I saw a girl I didn't recognise. She looked terrible and I was worried she might have got back on the gear.

'Hi, you alright?' I asked.

'Dunno. Want a drink, coffee?'

'Yeh why not.'

We walked to the front but our usual haunt was full of bikers.

'Never mind, I have tea in the flat,' she offered, and we strolled to her place.

Inside I noticed a picture of Charley on the bedside table. On the back was a phone number. I recognised the handwriting. It was Charley's. The number was hers too, or to be more precise it was the telephone number of Patrick's house. I went cold.

I quickly stuffed the photo in my shorts and drank my tea in silence. We eventually talked about the other night and how drunk I was. I was amazed to learn that I'd professed my undying love for Kat, told her I wanted to make love to her so badly and various other snippets of a night I had no recollection of at all.

We left friends but it was strained. I told her I was too old for her and perhaps she should look for a nice young lad to go out with instead, now she was clean. It didn't go down that well but what the hell was I supposed to say? I was still so naïve as far as women were concerned. Definitely another species, I was still discovering.

Twenty Eight

What Kat hadn't bothered to tell me was it was her who was in love with me. Not the other way around. Thinking back to a hundred or more compliments, a thousand smiles, looks, touches and sneaky glances I realised how stupid I'd been.

I always assumed I was unattractive. Big and ugly most people said. Why would anyone vaguely nice ever be interested in me? Once again I'd shown myself to have absolutely no concept of how a woman's mind worked or what things they liked. Strange that with guys I knew exactly what to expect. If they were a threat, whether they were carrying a weapon, if they were fast, strong or just tough as nails? I could read them like a book but with girls I may as well have been flicking through the pages of a quantum physics manual written in Serbo-Croat.

As far as Kat was concerned I was about the only human being who'd ever shown her any kindness, and so I suppose it was inevitable that in some way she would feel a certain affection towards me. Especially after I'd helped get her straight.

I should have noticed. I should have seen her face change when we met up again a few weeks later and I told her all about Charley, casual like.

'Look, she was my girlfriend, a long time ago. Another life.'

'Did you love her?'

'Yes, very much so.'

'What happened then?'

'She died.'

161

'Oh shit, I'm sorry Paul. Really I am.'

'It was a long time ago. Another coffee?'

'Yes please.'

I watched, I studied. I tried so hard but it was no good. I was sat opposite, armed with a milkshake and a teacake. Only about three feet away yet could I decipher the changing expressions on her face? Could I hell? I wanted benediction, a small sign that we were okay. Kat mopped vanilla ice cream from her lips with a serviette and smiled.

'So that photo you had? You didn't do anything?'

'Wha' do ya mean?'

'The phone number on the back.'

'I didn't really notice, I was just angry, sorry I took it...'

'Did you ring that number?'

'No, of course not!'

'Alright, I just need to know that's all.'

*

Satisfied she was telling the truth I relaxed a little and things went back to normal for a few days. Then I noticed Kat in the pub one night talking to a guy who was chatting her up.

With the same deadpan face she had displayed to me I listened to her explaining the virtues of lesbian love and how, being a bank manager, that this young lad couldn't possibly afford her, even if she did fancy trying a bloke for a laugh.

So I guess what eventually played out was all my

own doing. If I'd known she had written Patrick's number down. If I ever imagined, in a million years, that she'd be so stupid. That she might call his house and leave her own number, albeit the payphone at the bottom of the stairs, I would have probably strangled the bitch. Trouble was I had no idea what she'd done until it was too late.

The genie was now out of the lamp. Jack was out of his box. He couldn't be stuffed back inside and I was now, as they say in the business, seriously fucked.

Twenty Nine

Patrick was using heavy again. He was also drinking far too much vodka, not just at night, but throughout the day. Morgan had noticed but daren't say anything to her dad in case he flew into a violent rage and threatened to kick her out of the house again. However, after last week's outburst, when he'd called her a slut just like her mother, she'd finally had enough.

Morgan had never been close to her father. He'd always seemed so distant. Like he was somewhere else. She couldn't recall him ever playing with her when she was a toddler and he was never around to read her a bedtime story.

She remembered an ornate wooden trunk full of dolls and toys. She loved her beautiful house with its large garden and she enjoyed going out to eat. She had even learnt which knife and fork to use at a very early age.

At five years old she was packed off to an expensive private school, about a year after her mother had died. It broke her heart but also made her.

On term breaks she was looked after by a Spanish nanny, Maria, who was very kind but it wasn't the same. She used to get picked up from school by one of daddy's large friends in a posh car. Sat alone in the back seat she would regard her friends out of the tinted windows. They all seemed to have mummies and daddies who gave them hugs and kisses.

Her daddy only gave her a kiss when he gave her a present at Christmas and on her birthday. As the years went by she wasn't sure if she could remember what her mummy smelled like anymore.

Although she'd only been very young when Charley had got shot by that traitorous Welshman, she still recalled little things. And the photographs had helped keep her mother's memory alive as well. She often rummaged through the shoebox she kept hidden under the bed. If Patrick shouted at her or when she felt especially sad she would retreat to her room and carefully take out her most treasured possession, an old torn photograph of her mother.

It was about three inches by four and had been ripped down the middle. There was an arm across her mother's shoulder but it didn't show who the other figure in the frame was. Her mother had obviously fallen out with the mystery man or not wanted anyone to know who he was for whatever reason.

*

Morgan had been told to go to her room to study. She was doing her A levels next year and dad wouldn't be happy if all the cash he was spending on her education didn't pay dividends. Bored with the huge economics textbook she was reading, Morgan decided to get a bite to eat. She slowly opened the door to her bedroom and was just about to go downstairs when she heard her dad's raised voice.

'Look you cunt, if this is him, I want him dead. Do you understand?'

'Yes boss but...' stammered Michael.

'No ifs or buts. Do you hear me? Dead I said.'

'Okay boss, I'll take care of it but I was just going to say...'

'Say what?' snarled Patrick.

Michael lowered his voice and Morgan had to struggle to hear his reply.

'Well, what if she finds out? I mean he is her...'

Patrick punched Michael in the face and he rocked on his heels but didn't go down. The old Patrick would have floored him but he'd become weaker with all the white nose powder he was getting through, and he knew it. Although he was his longest-serving, most trusted right-hand man he still despised Michael more than most. He knew the truth about Paul and Charley and although they never spoke of it Patrick often thought he should kill him, just to shut him up.

'Sorry boss. I don't want you making a mistake, that's all. Something you might regret later.'

'I won't. And I'm not telling you again. Never ever speak of that Welsh man to me again. Now get it done. Use Seamus.'

Thirty

I'd heard it said that your life flashes before you when you know you're going to die. I don't know about that but one thing I do know is that your pulse races, adrenaline floods into your bloodstream and everything becomes crystal clear.

In that brief moment of realisation, a split second after a nerve impulse travelling at over one hundred miles per hour reached my brain, I had visions of riding a red tricycle up and down the broken paving slabs outside an old terraced house in south Wales.

I saw the mud-splattered, shabby cobs who lived in the overgrown field behind my home. I recalled how we used to jump on their backs and kick and squeeze their ribs like in the John Wayne films.

I tasted my first kiss, up against the zinc-roofed garages in the quarry, I remembered the city lights on the Taff, sparkling like stars, and the restful swell of the Celtic Sea, down west on a sultry August night, slowly washing over me…

I used to think that the end of the world was anywhere south of Pontypridd. That the scent of ashtrays, stale lager and cold lino was a happy home…

Charley was smiling now. Laughing at me and making me feel warm. Wrapped up in wanted…

The pain was sharp and instant, but not as bad as I thought it would be. It felt like I'd been hit by a car as the bullet struck me hard in the chest and I immediately fell backwards. My skull cracked on the tarmac and my eyes closed.

I feel myself slowly leave my body as a warm trickle of blood seeps through my fingers. My hand had instinctively flown to the point of impact and I'd gripped my jacket tight. Hand on heart I lay still and waited. It can't be long now? The whack in the forehead, which would finally end this feeling of being in limbo I'd had to live with for so many years. Maybe another few plugs in the chest for good luck? Not the bollocks I hoped.

I'd heard that a feeling of paralysis was common. That you lost the feeling in your legs and the ability to speak. I suddenly had a raging thirst. Probably the adrenaline coursing through my veins, perhaps the long day in the sun, the few drinks catching up with me too?

My mind had gone entirely empty now, like someone had switched a light off in my head. I was lying perfectly still, eyes shut tight and seemed to be floating away from the rushing night. I must have lost consciousness about then as I don't remember much else.

Thirty One

Back in London Patrick picks up the phone. There is a pause, then a brief beeping sound followed by Seamus's thick accent after he's pushed a few coins in the slot.

'Seamus, is that you?'

'Yes boss.'

'Well, is it done?'

'Yes boss.'

'Deadly. Okay, don't hang about, get back here before you grab some black stuff.'

'Aye boss, already in motorway services, payphone. Left an hour ago.'

'Fierce, good lad,' Patrick was clearly delighted.

Although it wasn't particularly safe in his patch at that time Patrick ignores everyone's advice and celebrates by going on a major bender. Michael and two of the other lads have to accompany him but Michael is not happy. Paul and him were good mates and he felt terrible he hadn't done more to try to talk Patrick out of sending the assassin to Wales.

They move on to Soho. They pass the Raymond Revue nightclub, which had closed a few months earlier, and find a strip club that Patrick liked where the girls would do extras if you stuffed a few more twenties in their knickers.

'Boss seems happy?' says Karl, a local lad from Tottenham, who was now working for the gang.

'Aye, don't take a lot these days, a big pair of Bristols and he's laughing,' replied Michael.

'You okay Mike?'

Michael hated being called Mike.

'Yeh mate, just wonder what the feck we're doing sometimes.'

Michael didn't like Karl much. He considered him a loud mouth and too loose with information.

'Havin' a laugh, innit.'

As the night wears on Michael starts to re-evaluate his own life. About how, on the one hand, he didn't know any other way to earn a living, but also, on the other hand, that the game was changing. And changing fast.

'Hey look, she's got her hand in his trousers now,' said Karl smirking.

'And?'

'Well, she's giving him a Tommy Tank innit.'

Michael couldn't have cared less.

*

After a week of being out on the lash Michael was beginning to get seriously pissed off with the boss now. The pattern was the same. Local boozer, few drinks accompanied by a few lines. Then into a club, a girl or two and then more drink and drugs, followed by some food and the odd scrap before a ride home in one of the lads' cars at dawn.

On the seventh day Michael really needed a rest. Apart from Patrick getting off his face the pub was quiet. They move on to one of the firm's own nightclubs. Morale in the gang isn't good at the moment and familiarity breeds contempt. Doing the same thing day after day, night after night makes you predictable. Predictable is not good.

The protection becomes sloppy. Michael and Karl are fed up with the way things are going again so eventually leave Patrick, apart from one minder, in a club out towards Hackney. He's mouthing off and trying to start a fight. A bad move in hindsight as the uneasy truce between the Irish and the Jamaican mob wasn't about to hold forever, especially with all the recent rumours of a new and violent Turkish mafia trying to muscle in as well.

About forty-five minutes after Michael had left the club, across the bar, nods were seen and winks acknowledged. A couple of hasty phone calls were made and in no time at all a posse of four large West Indian lads were swiftly escorting a shocked Patrick to a filthy alley behind his favourite nightspot for a game of punch whitey.

Patrick's bodyguard was lucky. He was ushered out the back door and shot in the back of the head. He never knew what hit him.

A van was backed up and a half-conscious Patrick was thrown in the back. At a nearby warehouse they spent about half an hour turning him into the Elephant Man before getting bored. Then someone suggested an iron. His screams amused them for a while but time was getting on and business was business.

In the end there was no panache, no witty remarks, just cold steel that penetrated stomach, kidneys and spleen multiple times. He bled out in less than fifteen minutes.

*

171

Morgan was crying. Not because the house was going mental with people shouting out obscene threats of revenge all over the place. No. She didn't give a monkey's that her vicious father had just been carved up and his body dumped on the doorstep of one of their pubs.

She cried because she was entirely alone now. She never wanted to get involved in the family business and now had no reason to stick around. She was a well-educated young woman, had a wardrobe full of designer clothes, was confident and beautiful. She didn't take shit from anyone, growing up surrounded by hard men as she had been. She had enough cash in her trust fund to last most women a dozen lifetimes. She had no reason to stay but she did want answers. Answers to questions that had played on her mind her whole life.

She had to speak to Michael.

Thirty Two

For a few days there was relative calm. There was no obvious successor to Patrick's firm although a few rival Irish families had sent sympathies along with the biggest bunches of flowers you'd ever seen. Maybe they were looking to merge firms, or perhaps more likely, to takeover what was left of the business.

It was 2004 and the whole criminal scene was changing, especially in London. The old school mantra of honour amongst thieves was long gone. The new players were all foreign – Bengalis, Chinese, Albanians, Jamaicans and Russians to mention just a few of the new breed. It wasn't an environment Michael wanted to play a further part in either.

After Patrick's funeral it was decided that Morgan should get out of town for a bit until things were sorted out. There was all hell about to break loose now the other gangs sensed a vacuum forming. There were the Kurdish rivals to the Turks, the blacks of course plus the Pakistani's and Bangladeshi's, all vying for position and the lion's share of the lucrative heroin and crack trade.

Morgan didn't need a second telling.

'I'll go to the beach, down west Wales,' she blurts out.

'Aye, alright love, we'll have a couple of boys go with you though,' says Michael. 'Just in case, but I'm sure it'll be fine,' he was trying to reassure himself as much as Morgan.

'No, it's fine. I can stay with one of my friend's from boarding school. She has a farm down there, a few miles after Cardigan, plenty of security too,' she lied easily through steely blue eyes.

Michael stuttered a reply, 'I'd still be happier if you had a few of our lads…'

Morgan interrupted, 'No, I'll be grand but can I ask you something before I go though?'

'Yeh of course you can,' he smiled warmly before nearly choking on a mouthful of lager as Morgan pulls out a faded old photograph and pushes it in front of Michael's dropping jaw.

'Tell me. And I'll know if you're telling fibs. Who is the other person in this picture Michael?'

Thirty Three

Morgan gets off the train in Cardiff Central station, adjusts her Ray Bans, walks regally down the steps like a Vogue cover girl on location and once outside immediately hops into a taxi, placing her Prada overnight bag next to her on the seat.

The Asian driver looks in the mirror and asks where she wants to go.

'Porthcawl,' comes the confident reply and Morgan leans back in the seat.

It takes about an hour to travel the thirty miles of mostly motorway plus a few minor roads. She makes the taxi driver's week when she tips him a fiver on top of the fare and checks into the Seabank Hotel.

Originally built as a house in 1854 it served as a boys boarding school before eventually becoming a hotel in the 1920s. A quick shower and a change of clothes is followed by a cheese and onion sandwich and a drink.

Sipping her gin and tonic Morgan looks out at the panoramic views of the Bristol Channel that stretch all the way down to Swansea Bay. In her hand she turns over and over an old photograph and on the bar is a scrap of paper with an address written on it in Karl's untidy handwriting.

Morgan needs some fresh air and the short walk into town is just what she needs to clear her head. She adjusts her sunglasses and looks across the sparkling bay, a light breeze, warm on her face.

Passing the crumbling façade of the Grand Pavilion she negotiates a cluster of pigeons that are swiftly chased away by a much larger herring gull. The spoils, a tray of half-eaten chips, go to him alone.

Morgan is soon stood outside a run-down house in Esplanade Avenue. The door is finally answered after three knocks.

'May I come in? I want to talk to you about... my father,' says Morgan.

'How did you find me?' slurs Kat as she stands back to allow Morgan to enter the dingy flat.

'Contact in the police,' she lies.

Kat looks sheepish and scans her own room for obvious contraband.

'I haven't done anything, honest love.'

'Relax. I'm not here about you. Tell me about him?' she says, holding up the torn photo of her mum and pointing to the huge arm wrapped around her.

Kat gets defensive.

'How do I know who that is? You can't even see him.'

'Look again. There is a large raised scar on the arm. Recognise it?'

Kat did. She had spent the last few years holding on to it, running her small fingers along the pink and white line that dissected a forest of arm hair. Then she got scared.

This young woman looked dangerous. Maybe she wasn't his child after all. Maybe she was here to tidy up loose ends. Kat had heard about these people from London. Paul had even told her a few stories when he was drunk. Suddenly she lost it.

'Fuck off, fuck off! Get out!' she screamed at the

top of her voice but Morgan didn't budge an inch. She just stared harder at the broken young woman sat next to her.

'He's dead! Happy now?' said Kat.

'Was he the guy who was killed?' now it was Morgan's turn to get upset.

She stood to leave but Kat grabbed her hand. 'Wait. I have some things.'

Kat fell on to the floor and dragged a small cardboard box from under the bed. 'Here, take them. I can't look at them anymore.'

*

Back in her hotel room Morgan tipped the box of meagre possessions onto the bed. There were beermats with writing scribbled on, a few postcards, a couple of pieces of cheap jewellery, half a dozen corks from wine bottles, leaflets from Welsh tourist attractions and a small bundle of photos. She flicked through the pile and saw her mother, smiling back at her, quite clearly happy. She had a sparkle in her eye and the widest grin.

She thought about the portraits she had of Charley back in her London bedroom. Posed and professional but no matter how good the photographer was he couldn't put in what was missing. In those shots her mother was beautiful. She was dressed in smart outfits, she'd had her hair done and wore a hint of makeup. Stunning yes, but not genuinely happy. Not like these images. She seemed carefree, and if Morgan had to bet, madly in love with whoever was taking the pictures.

She soon found the image she was looking for. The same photo she had treasured all those years but this time intact. She ran her fingers over the smiling face of a man she assumed she'd never known but then all of a sudden it hit her. She did know him. He was the man she'd played with as a child. The one who was always with Michael. He used to tickle her with his big fat fingers. Make her laugh and pick her up and throw her into the air when no-one was around. He'd push her really high on the swing and fetch her drinks and crisps. Morgan always believed she had a real life teddy bear, her very own big friendly giant from one of her fairy tale picture books.

When she opened her eyes the pillow was soaking wet with tears and Morgan sniffed the cold cotton. She must have fallen asleep for a moment. Exhausted by the discovery of who exactly her real father was. The big Welsh man, Paul. She put two and two together. So he was the one she'd been told had killed her mother. The one whose evil image she'd imagined, created as a child. She hadn't made the connection. Out of the blue it all made sense.

Although confused and angry she now realised that in the space of a week she had lost two fathers. One she still hated and one she'd hated all her life until a few moments ago.

In fact Paul was doubtless her favourite person, apart from her mother, when she was little. He always had time for her, never got angry and always smiled at her. She had to find out what happened. And she had a bone to pick with Michael too.

He'd told her not to bother with any fool's errand,

said it would only upset her and might be dangerous. Michael had confessed to Morgan that her real dad was from Wales but said that he'd disappeared years ago and no-one knew where he was. Anything to stop her coming here it seemed.

Thirty Four

The following morning Morgan was hammering on Kat's bedsit door again. On her second visit she took in her surroundings in a bit more detail. She couldn't help notice that every surface had a grubby stain upon it. There was a thick layer of dust on everything else. The fusty room smelled of cigarettes and mould.

Although Morgan had been brought up in relative luxury, with a silver spoon in her mouth, she'd never fitted in at the posh private school she attended and often got into fights with the other girls. It didn't take her long to establish her position in the pecking order though as she quickly shut up anyone who questioned her funny accent or gave her a sideways look that she didn't appreciate. She may have looked like a princess clad in designer outfits from Paris and Milan with a brand new Patek Philippe Twenty-4 on her wrist but cross her at your peril. There was an inner strength and resilience that even she had no idea where it came from.

Morgan knocked again and heard movement behind the door as the floorboards creaked.

'Wha' da you want?' slurred Kat, obviously half-cut even at this early hour.

'Just a few more questions, I won't be long.'

The door groaned on its hinges.

'Okay, come in and grab a pew.'

Morgan kicked an empty can of Strongbow out of the way, brushed a few crumbs from the soiled bedspread and sat down.

'Wanna brew?'

'No thank you. I only want to know how they found him?'

'I dunno. Fuck off. Leave me alone.'

Morgan flipped. She was in no mood to be messed around by this lowlife trash. She lashed out, quickly grabbing Kat's ponytail and twisting her hair around her own arm.

'Ow, stop, you're hurting me,' the shorter girl shouted.

'How did they know where to come bitch?'

Kat started to cry. 'I was jealous alright! I didn't mean to do anything. I loved him. Honest I did...'

Morgan slowly released her grip and scanned the filthy room. In the corner, under the window she noticed a syringe with blood in it. She shuddered inside.

She sat and stared at Kat for the last time. Rage building up inside her as she watched her sob herself into a state; arms folded tight about her skinny frame in a defensive gesture.

This stupid slag had got her father killed. She thought she wanted answers but suddenly she didn't need to know any more. He was gone and it was this stupid junkie's fault. She wanted to kill her. Take a knife and plunge it right through her heart, but then another notion crossed her mind.

'Here, have yourself a party on me,' said Morgan standing and opening the door to the stairwell. She tossed a hundred quid in notes on the threadbare carpet and laughed as she watched Kat throw herself on top of the money and frantically scoop it up.

Thirty Five

Strange rumours had quickly spread around town that a gunman had killed someone. No-one knew where the story had first come from but it must be true as everyone was talking about it. The latest version had it down as a drug deal gone wrong. It must have been, as Porthcawl was a fairly trouble-free sort of town. Fights on a Saturday outside the nightclub but nothing too tasty.

There was nothing in the local paper but that didn't mean a thing. The journalists were half asleep down here and the police weren't to be trusted either. Perhaps they were even in on it?

Various places had been suggested as the execution spot. Loud-mouthed experts on gang warfare started emerging from every pub in town as the beer went down. Spatters of blood from various weekend scuffles were found all over the streets and all had been proposed as possible sites for the deed, although they were all wrong of course.

Nobody had noticed the very small, dark red stain on the edge of the car park near the rundown façade of the old Victorian seafront. Soon though, it too became yesterday's news, part of ancient folklore, like the live bands and wild parties at the old Knights Arms.

*

Kat was stood outside a kebab shop a few yards off the front. She'd been thrown out of Streets, the nightclub on John Street for trying to pickpocket a girl in the toilets and wasn't sure where she should go now.

'Alright love? You lost?' asked a drunken youth, who'd just emerged from a nearby alley. He carried on doing his fly up as Kat replied.

'Fuck off, leave me alone' she said through night-grey eyes.

'Okay, keep your fuckin' hair on. I wouldn't touch you with his,' the clubber said, pointing to a friend who was waiting for him.

The lads walked off giggling, in search of a burger.

Kat strolled towards the lighthouse on the breakwater, passing the Pier Hotel on the way. Oblivious to the bother she'd caused there.

A stag party of boys reeled past her going the other way. One of them was wet. Soaked to the skin, hair matted to his head, his thin trousers showing all he had.

'Fancy a fuck love?' one of the boys shouted.

'It's his birthday. And the dull sod is getting hitched,' cried another.

Kat ignored them and walked on.

The gang of boys soon met a gang of girls outside the chippy. Obscene t-shirts mingled with pink balloons and dangling dildos. A marriage made in heaven.

A few minutes later a dealer Kat knew rescued her from the tempting prospect of the cold ocean. Scurrying back to her flat one of her shoes fell off. She didn't bother to stop and pick it up but carried on running as the clock tower chimed.

In the safety of her squalor the blood from her cut foot seeped into the bedsit's fetid wool carpet. The tiny room smelled of ash and peanuts. Choking, stuffy air. In the days that followed it would become infected and make it agony to walk on.

The remains of the town's partygoers found taxis, hotels and caravans.

As Kat snored through the dawn she dreamed about her Prince Charming. It was a wonderful dream, one she had often. It seeped in, refreshed her, but when she opened her eyes he'd vanished like always.

Deep down in her heart she knew he was gone and it made her unbelievably sad.

Thirty Six

It didn't take many days before she was hooked again. The guilt never left her.

'It's the loneliness that really gets to me,' said Kat.

'You're not lonely babe, you got me,' said her dealer.

'When you realise that the only good thing in your life is gone and worse still, it was all your fault.'

A scabby tattooed arm tried to comfort her.

'Nothing I can say to myself will change the way I feel. I have nobody left now...'

'Here, this one is on the house. Let's go back to your place for a bit shall we?' said the pusher as he closed Kat's fingers around a small plastic bag he'd placed in her cold hand.

When the chips were down in a previous existence Kat had one person who still had faith in her. For four years Paul had been there for her. He fed and watered her, he got her to face up to her demons and was the most patient, beautiful man she'd ever know.

As the smack rushed through her veins she meditated on his shining blue eyes, his striking, rugged features, his incredible physique, his generosity, his wonderful sense of humour...

And she'd repaid him by being a reckless, selfish cow who'd got him killed. She had lost all hope and now had no reason to keep living.

She was just another statistic for the *Twin Town* generation. Like a silent movie star she was tied to the railway line, waiting for a train that was hurtling down the tracks at breakneck speed.

A month after Morgan's visit, broke and addicted she was selling herself again. Not that she ever did much trade looking the way she did now. Progressing to crack wasn't really a great career choice either.

Two months on and she was discovered bleeding from a head wound, draped over the wrought-iron railings in the local park. She got emergency treatment, got patched up at taxpayers expense, was enrolled on a drug's programme and then let loose back into the community.

She never turned up to the rehab clinic. It took another couple of weeks before social services wondered what had become of her. Different agencies were alerted. Pieces of paper were sent backward and forward to different departments and managers agreed that something should be done. Priorities were identified and decisions made in various meetings.

A few days later Kat was found dead in her flat after neighbours complained about the smell.

Thirty Seven

'What the fuck?' It's dark but not exactly black. I can feel small lumps of gravel digging into the back of my head, my toes seem to be moving and a gallon and a half of blood appears to be pumping furiously around the inside of my body, not outside it. My chest hurts but the bleeding has stopped.

I'm trying to recall who I am, where I am, but my mind is blank. It's like I've just woken from a coma. I really don't want to but I force myself to open my eyes. Everything is blurred and my hands start to shake. I look around but I'm alone. The shooter has gone.

It's about twenty minutes after the biggest adrenaline rush of my life. I try to stand but my shaky legs won't work. I turn myself over onto all fours and throw up. For no apparent reason I feel like I want one of those super-sweet sugary doughnuts you get at the fair.

*

After a minute of panic, confusion and disbelief I run my hands over my upper body and notice that I have a small hole in my denim jacket, about where my heart would be. Then I open the flap on my breast pocket and stick my hand in.

'Ouch, shit!'

I slowly pull out a bloody finger, a few pieces of jagged metal and realise that's where my new iPhone was.

'The future is fuckin' bright,' I say out loud, then start laughing in between retching.

A nervous laugh followed by more nausea.

Rubbing my hand over my chest in disbelief I can't find any injuries at all. As I try to walk my breath catches with each movement. Possibly broke a rib or two.

'Happy days. Right, let's go get a friggin' doughnut.'

Thirty Eight

It was a tough decision to make but I felt I had no choice. I dusted myself down and started to jog to the Rock Hotel. I knew the landlord well and knew if there was one person I could trust it was Gwyn.

I snuck in via the back door and quickly spilled out some of my story. I gave Gwyn the key to my flat and told him I needed a big favour. After he'd found my stash of money I told him to divide it in two. One half was for him, the other to be sent on to me, when I rang him in the week with my new address that would be a pub in which I could safely watch the postman do his duty from a safe distance.

I told him to take anything else he wanted, then turn the place over, smash a few things, pull out the drawers, turn the chairs over before leaving and then throw the key away. Make it look like someone had robbed the place.

A born storyteller I couldn't have chosen a better accomplice to weave a convincing tale of my violent demise. I needed the locals, the pub gossips and any Irish eavesdroppers, even poor Kat, to be under no illusion of what had happened.

I was dead. Shot at point blank range, straight through the heart, died instantly. A local gang found me, and they figured it would be best all round if they rapidly disposed of my body on a local farm. In case the cops were trying to set them up for the hit or something. No-one would miss me so what difference did it make? Well, only Kat perhaps, but she had a big gob and I couldn't

189

risk her blabbing to anyone, no matter how innocently.

Gwyn convinced me he would keep to his half of the bargain. The few grand gift I was offering him would certainly help and he also wasn't stupid. He knew if he cocked this up and I survived long enough to find out he would be paid a visit in the wee hours. It was a huge gamble but I had to take it. I figured I had a fifty-fifty chance of pulling it off and those were odds I was more than happy to take. Especially after the million to one lottery I'd just won first prize in.

I left as quietly as I'd arrived all those years ago. I pulled the collar up on my tatty denim and stuck a black woollen cap on my head that I pinched from the backroom of the pub. I walked past the park and managed to get the last bus back to Pontypridd station. I then took a stroll towards Hopkinstown and headed north up the valley. As I walked alongside the River Rhondda I thought of an old book I'd read. It was about how a man is drawn upstream to rescue another who's gone crazy.

By two o'clock in the morning I'd navigated Porth, avoided the dregs being chucked out of the clubs and headed for an old friend's house in Trealaw to lay low for a few days.

I spent the time wondering if anyone would be sent to rescue me or if I would die here.

Thirty Nine

Morgan had arrived in Porthcawl a couple of weeks after the botched assassination attempt. She stood out from the crowd in this small seaside town and her trawl of the pubs and cafés only brought her suspicious looks and silence.

The address she'd got from Karl was her only clue. She knew he wouldn't understand the significance and knew Michael was holding back something. After the funeral, he'd only told her that Patrick wasn't her real dad. Long gone, no idea where he is, were his words. But he wouldn't say anything else.

Dull as fuck Karl was a different matter. The roids had obviously gone to his head and killed the last few brain cells off. Morgan turned the charm on and he'd told her he wasn't supposed to say anything. She smiled again. Then he did. Perhaps he supposed he might ingratiate himself with the former boss's daughter?

Anyway, the story was her mum's killer was hiding out in Porthcawl and he'd been taken out on Patrick's orders. Morgan had already worked out he was her dad but wanted to know for sure. Quizzing Karl further he told her that not everyone believed this bloke was as guilty as they said but Patrick was determined. She decided she would make a small detour seeing as she'd told Michael she was travelling to Tenby then Cardiganshire. It was on the way.

*

Locals had heard the tittle-tattle and wanted to know who this classy, but obviously bold as brass teenage bird was asking questions about a bloke no one seemed to know.

She had a photo of a man and a woman with her and people thought she might be related. Best keep quiet. Foreigners from England weren't exactly unwelcome in these particular hillsides but her posh voice with a hint of an exotic accent worried people. She didn't fit in so best stay schtum.

After no luck visiting all the drinking dens in town Morgan was about ready to give up and bugger off down west for a week or so. Then she decided, seeing as she was down here anyway, she'd just as well try the outskirts too. Maybe her dad had been careful. Maybe he only drank in certain pubs he knew to be safe. You couldn't exactly miss him, the size of him, but the locals weren't saying anything.

'What can I get you love?' asked Gwyn.

Morgan was about to blurt out "champagne" but stopped herself. 'Cider please. A half.'

The bar was deserted apart from an old guy scanning the racing page of The Sun in the corner. She started making small talk with the barman and after a few sips of her drink she pulled out the photo and placed it on the bar.

She watched closely as Gwyn, the landlord of the Rock Hotel, looks fleetingly at the smiling faces then shakes his head. That was quick, she thought. Acting nervously Morgan is convinced he knows something. He recognises them. She decides to go for broke.

'I've been all over town for practically a week now.

Nobody is telling me the truth. They say they don't know this man but I know they do.'

'Sorry love, can't help you,' says Gwyn and turns to walk away.

'He was my dad.'

Gwyn stops in his tracks and slowly turns back to face this stunning young beauty in front of him. He rapidly recovers his composure.

'I can ask around love but I don't know him. Leave a number perhaps.'

Morgan scribbles a mobile number down on a piece of paper she retrieves from her handbag and hands it to Gwyn. As he tries to take it she holds on and looks him straight in the eyes.

'The few people who have told me anything say this man might have been the one who was shot here a while back.'

'Aye I heard something about that,' says Gwyn.

'So who you gonna call if he's dead? Ghostbusters?'

Gwyn went white as Morgan slowly smiled to herself. She still wasn't one hundred per cent sure but it was a glimmer of hope.

'Describe me to him. Let him know Patrick is dead. And don't lose my number. I'll be back.'

*

Although they didn't frequent his pub Gwyn had seen her sort before. The local convent school had girls like that. Tall, slim, beautiful. Confidence bordering on arrogance.

He didn't like them one bit but this one was different. He watches as the most elegant underage drinker he'd ever seen walks out of the pub. Cursing to himself he's not sure what to do. He waits for half an hour, paces up and down the bar before finally plucking up the courage to ring the number he has behind the bar. It came on a postcard a few days earlier. Just in case anyone came looking he was to phone Paul and warn him.

'Hi Paul, I have something to tell you. I think you should know anyway.'

After relaying the story there is silence on the other end of the phone.

'Sounds like a trap Gwyn, I don't have any kids.'

'She said for me to describe her to you.'

'Mmm, not sure that would help… shit, wait. Did she leave a name?'

'Aye, Morgan.'

'Fuck. Okay, thanks mate.'

Click.

Forty

Morgan was packed and ready to leave. Her taxi was booked for two o'clock that afternoon. Before leaving for Tenby she phoned home and began the interrogation.

'Michael, is that you? It's me.'

'Hi love, are you alright? I was worried about you.'

'No need, I told you. Been horse riding with my friend Mel, down the beach, on the sands, having a fab time.'

'When you were growing up I could always tell when you were telling porkies,' said Michael. 'Your voice goes up an octave.' He laughed.

'Lucky guess.'

'Where are you?'

'I think he might be alive.'

Silence.

'Who?'

'You know who, why didn't you tell me?'

There is more quiet on the other end of the line.

'I'm sorry love, I tried to stop Patrick but he was obsessed...'

'I thought you two were friends?'

'We were, I'm sorry I thought it was better if you didn't know. You'd lost one dad, I couldn't tell you they were killing the other one too. Shit, I'm so sorry Morgan.'

'Yeh but he might still be alive...'

'No way. Seamus is pretty reliable... shit sorry love.'

'Forget it. Look, it's a long shot but I just have a feeling. Trust me.'

Michael was stuttering on the phone and Morgan guessed he was feeling guilty.

'Shit.'

The penny dropped.

'What's up Michael?'

'Oh nothing love. Look, take care. Don't get your hopes up though, okay?'

'I'll be fine.'

*

Morgan didn't want to leave but felt she'd done all she could for the time being. Gwyn wasn't in the pub when she'd returned and the barmaid said he'd gone on holidays to his caravan but couldn't tell her where that was or when he might be back. She'd added that he sometimes went for the whole winter and they didn't have phones there.

What could she do on her own? She decided to walk through the town centre one last time.

As she strolled down the small incline into town she couldn't believe her eyes. There were five Elvis Presley's walking towards her. Two had guitars under their arms but all of them were covered, head to toe, in rhinestone jumpsuits, open down to the waist.

'Afternoon missy,' the first Elvis touched his quiff as he passed.

'Thank you very much,' said the others in unison.

What kind of weird place is this?

The Elvis Festival, which runs every September, attracts tribute artists and devotees from across the world and is now recognized as the biggest gathering of Elvis fans in Europe and maybe in the world.

It was all too surreal for Morgan. She needed a drink.

Forty One

'Yeh, speak,' said Michael.

There was a long pause from the caller.

'Okay, stop playing silly buggers, who is it?'

'Hi Michael,' I said and waited.

'Fuckin' hell, is that you Paul?'

'Aye mate. I had a visitor recently mind you. Not a particularly genial person shall we say. But I'm sure you'd know all about that wouldn't you?' I let the menace hang for a moment...

'Oh man, Paul I had no choice. I tried to talk him out of it, I swear I did. He was a nutter, you know that...'

I heard the panic in Michael's voice but I wasn't going to stop yet. The least I could do was put the shits up him for a while.

'I see the phone is still by that big old kitchen window Michael me old mucker. You're lit up rather nicely there in the morning sun.'

I watched, then laughed, as Michael's head cocked to the side, like a dog listening for a car door slam which signals its owner's return. Then he hits the deck.

'Okay, stop pissing about,' Michael was starting to regain his cool.

'You gonna invite me in then or what?'

'Do I want to?'

'Yeh, you're alright. Am I though?'

He hadn't changed a bit. Maybe a bit fatter but still the same old paddy twat I'd come to respect and admire back in the day.

Michael poured us each a large glass of malt and

198

observed me intently before speaking.

'Paul. I know I should have tried to do more. To warn you even but Patrick wouldn't tell me where you were until it was done. I think he guessed I might blab. Honest mate I tried for years to get him to forget about you...'

'Who was he anyway?' I interrupted.

'Who was who?'

'The gunman.'

'Oh, I see. A lad from the bog. West coast, extremely religious believe it or not. He's gone back there now.'

'So why didn't he make sure?'

'Fate? I don't know. When he turned up at the house I was sent away. No-one would tell me anything...'

'What do ya mean, fate?' I held the whiskey glass in my left hand and fidgeted my right inside my coat a little.

'Whoa. I don't know. Perhaps he thought one was enough? Perhaps he believed God was trying to tell him something?'

'Is he likely to come back? Finish the job like,' I asked.

'No, he wouldn't have left you alive unless he'd wanted to. He must have had a change of heart.'

'It was dark, perhaps he didn't realise?'

'Believe me. He changed his mind, don't know why but...'

I raised a hand to silence him. I guessed that Seamus must have been watching me for a while before he followed me back from the beach. Perhaps he saw something of himself? Perhaps one of the other boys had told him I wasn't such a bad lad? Maybe, when he'd realised the bullet had rebounded off the metal of my mobile he really did believe it was God's will? He didn't think it right to question that and simply walked away. He probably figured I'd do a runner and the warning would be enough for me to disappear forever. Nice lad.

'Look there's a few other things you don't know.'

'Go on...'

'The reason Charley came back to London. It wasn't 'cos she didn't love you, you know that right?'

'Well, I guess so but she wouldn't tell me. Just said it was safer me not knowing.'

'Patrick only wanted her so he'd look good. He threatened to hurt you if she didn't agree, even though he had no idea who you were back then.'

'So our meeting was just coincidence?'

'Yep. I don't normally believe in it but yes. Patrick had no idea who you were. Neither did I until I saw Charley's mood change. Then I had my suspicions.'

'So Morgan's really mine?'

'Yeh, apart from her mother only me and the boss knew she wasn't his but no-one had any idea who the real father was. And I convinced Patrick it best to forget about that.'

'Bloody hell. So if I hadn't joined your firm she'd still be alive? It was all my fault...

'No mate. You can't blame yourself. Patrick was the bad guy here, not you.'

'There's more isn't there?'

'Well, yeh. Charley found out who killed her dad. I

often wonder if that was why she came back. It was Frank, when he was a youngster, just starting out.'

'The decoy drugs raid?'

'You're catching on quick boyo. Yep, Charley set Frank up, made sure we were out of danger too. See, she was always looking out for you.'

'Shit.' I could feel myself filling up. Even after all these years the pain was still raw.

'How did Patrick get it?'

'Rival gang. It wasn't pleasant if it makes you feel any better.'

'Yeh a bit. Would have preferred to have had a few hours with him myself though.'

Michael was uneasy. He probably saw the anger swell up inside me. He didn't know I only had my fingers under my coat.

'Alright, what you wanna know buttie?' I asked.

'Only one thing,' he replied.

'And?'

'I just want to know. If you have to do it then do it but I don't want to spend my life running. Like you had to. I need to know mate.'

'Know what?' I said.

'I take it back. You always were a dull fucker! Am I a dead man or what, or can you ever forgive me?'

I let that last sentence hang in the air for a bit.

Michael stared at me and I stared back.

'Nothing to forgive mate.'

Forty Two

Michael phoned the hotel in Porthcawl and told Morgan to check back in for another few days. Said he might have some information coming through soon and it was best if she stayed in town for a while. She pleaded with him to tell her what he'd found out but he merely said sit tight.

The next day Morgan wasted the morning staring blankly out to sea. At lunch she spent far too long moving a delicious Glamorgan sausage around her plate. Perhaps the emotional turmoil of the last few weeks had finally caught up with her.

She drained the last of her orange juice and shook herself back to the present. She wasn't the sort of girl who let life wash over her. She was a go-getter. Like her mother before her she'd learnt that life didn't give you anything for free. You had to grab the bull by the horns. Snatch it when it came along.

Making sure her mobile was charged she decided to go for a walk on the beach while she waited for more news.

*

In The Ghetto was blasting out of a jukebox on the front. Crowds of drunken valley women, clad in sparkly costumes and silly cowboy hats were singing along, getting most of the words wrong. They twirled around, drinks in hand and danced in the street. Strings of plastic beads and garlands of rainbow-coloured flowers were draped around their necks as the lager flowed and the chanting increased.

The crooning continued as Morgan passed the Lifeboat pub and headed towards the fair at Coney Island. As she strolls through the gates she can still hear music playing loud, echoing across Sandy Bay. In front of her the heavens are wide and clear. There is a faint whisper of candyfloss cloud in the distance. Like a nomadic spirit crossing the blue-desert sky.

When she reaches the steps she skips down to the dull-gold sand and wanders without purpose towards the beckoning sea. The sound of the crowd partying in town drifts across the salty breeze. It would be a good night to be in Porthcawl if you had someone special to enjoy it with.

*

The tide was right out and it would be a long walk to reach the waves. Morgan didn't have anything better to do so she continued walking.

Stopping briefly she gazed down at a large jellyfish that had become stranded on the seashore. There must have been a storm out to sea last night.

Thinking about her own situation, Morgan knew she had to split. Get away from everything. Start afresh. She took a deep breath, filled her lungs with oxygen, and walked on.

When she got closer to the water's edge she sat down on the warm ground and let the soothing sound of lapping waves wash over her. The tide must have been turning because twenty minutes later her shoes got wet as the Bristol Channel reminded her nothing stays the same forever.

Jumping to her feet and stretching up to the sky Morgan turned away from the sea and thought she might as well go for a drink and join the party.

Before she got halfway back she realised she wasn't entirely alone on the shore. Someone appeared to be walking straight to her. She turned back to the water but saw no-one behind her. The large shape in front of her grew bigger.

Ambling towards her at first then slowly breaking into a jog.

*

Shimmering through the late afternoon heat haze I saw her silhouetted against the orange sun. Long-legged and slender, striking, even at a distance.

I stopped abruptly. I stood like a lone, weather-beaten tree in a vast open field. What was I supposed to do?

I hold out my arms and hope. Morgan runs but doesn't stop. She throws herself at me like an excited puppy. Wrapped around my chest like an octopus she squeezes tight and I feel her heavy breathing turn to sobs.

We walk back to the steps, my scarred arm cwtching her shoulders. Way out to sea a ship's horn emits a low moan.

Sitting on the wall together we talk. Easy and relaxed, like two old friends who'd just bumped into each other after half a lifetime apart. Our voices shred the silence of the deserted beach. The hum of distant pop music muted as the breeze changes direction.

I'm afraid to blink in case I miss something. Scared that my daughter might vanish into the air. Every second is more important than all that's gone before. I finally see light ahead in place of darkness.

An hour went by, then another. The passing of time was something that happened to other people. All sense of place abandoned. The fog started to lift from my heart. We turn towards the water. Fingers circled fingers, her delicate hand warm and safe in mine.

We watch the rust-red sun burn and shimmer, then finally disappear into the sage-green sea. Above our heads hangs the light from a fat milky moon.

Tomorrow I will see Porthcawl fade in the rear view mirror as we head towards a new life...

Somewhere that isn't here.

You may also like:

Ctrl-Alt-Delete
'The novel for the Facebook generation. An ambitious tour de force that should put Wales well and truly on the international crime thriller map. Believable characters and a gripping story. Can't wait for a sequel to find out what happens to Hal. Love the 'Alien' tag line too, very contemporary and quite scary.' – *Mark Jones*

Raising Skinny Elephants...
'Great sequel. I opted to read Ctrl-Alt-Delete again to get into the characters! Enjoyed it a second time around & couldn't wait to find time to read Raising Skinny Elephants. Thoroughly enjoyed, gutted when the book ended, great talented author, can't wait for his next book. – *clairy*

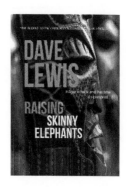

iCommand
'Absolutely amazing trilogy. Had me gripped from the very first book until the very end of the third, I could not put them down I just had to keep turning the page to find out what happened next. Would literally gasp out loud in public when a new plot twist would blow my mind. I've never read anything quite like it before, gripping is understatement, highly recommend' – *Nikohl Davies*

Published by

www.publishandprint.co.uk

Printed in Poland
by Amazon Fulfillment
Poland Sp. z o.o., Wrocław

63936241R00119